Josie gritted her teeth

"I suppose I may be allowed to own a house at twenty-three?"

"Certainly. But not the house next door. And in case you're going to say why not, it's because I shall own it myself in a few days. I plan to restore the villa to its former glory, to take down the dividing walls and replan the rooms."

"Really?" Josie raised delicate eyebrows. Leon was so confident, so disgustingly sure of himself that it would be a pleasure to take him down a peg or two. But she mustn't rush it.

Marjorie Lewty was born in Cheshire, England, and grew up between there and the Isle of Man. She moved to Liverpool and married there. Now widowed, she has a son who is an artist, and a married daughter. She has always been drawn to writing and started with magazine short stories, then serials and finally book-length romances, which are the most satisfying of all. Her hobbies include knitting, music and lying in the garden thinking of plots!

A Real
Engagement
Marjorie Lewty

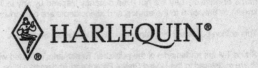

HARLEQUIN®

TORONTO • NEW YORK • LONDON
AMSTERDAM • PARIS • SYDNEY • HAMBURG
STOCKHOLM • ATHENS • TOKYO • MILAN • MADRID
PRAGUE • WARSAW • BUDAPEST • AUCKLAND

ISBN 0-373-17438-1

A REAL ENGAGEMENT

First North American Publication 1999.

Look us up on-line at: http://www.romance.net

Printed in U.S.A.

PROLOGUE

IT HAD all begun that June morning, when Charles—
her father liked her to call him Charles—had phoned
to invite her to lunch. 'I'm off to New York tomorrow, Jo, and there's a small matter of business to be
settled between us before I leave.' She had guessed
that it would have something to do with her mother's
will, details of which had not been finalised yet. 'And
I've got some news for you,' Charles had continued,
and his voice had sounded excited, almost euphoric.
'Twelve-thirty at Claridge's, OK? I'll send Baker with
the Rolls to pick you up.' He hadn't given her time
to reply.

So, at twelve-thirty that morning, Charles Dunn's
shining Rolls Royce had transported her to Claridges,
and now she was standing in the lounge looking for
Charles, her tall, slim figure, russet curls and greenish-
hazel eyes attracting covert glances from a party of
men at a nearby table.

Charles was sitting at a small table with a bottle of
champagne in a bucket beside him and two glasses
on the table. He stood up with his charming smile as
she joined him. He was putting on weight, she noticed, but he still looked as handsome as ever, immaculate in a grey pin-stripe suit with a camellia in
his buttonhole. He kissed her affectionately on the
cheek. 'Hullo, poppet. You're looking charming. I

like that green dress; it's new, isn't it? Sit down and join me in a celebration.'

She smiled back at him. He was her father and she loved him, in spite of the misery he had brought to her poor, sad mother.

'What are we celebrating, exactly?' she asked, accepting a glass of champagne.

Charles looked slightly abashed. 'I'm getting married.'

Josie's brows rose. 'For the fourth time?'

He fiddled with the stem of his glass. 'Well, you know how it is.'

She couldn't help laughing. 'I know how *you* are. OK, then, tell me all about it.'

Charles needed no encouragement. The story halted only briefly when they moved to the dining-room for lunch. Here, waiters glided noiselessly between tables where glass and cutlery gleamed on snowy damask cloths. Josie was hungry, and prepared to enjoy the smoked salmon with a promise of duckling to follow. Charles, however, only wanted to talk about his new love.

Josie had heard the same story twice before. The only difference was that this woman was American. Her name was Gabrielle and she was half-French. Divorced, of course, and very wealthy, Josie gathered. Not that that would matter much to Charles, whose thriving property business, together with various smaller concerns, had made him a very rich man. He must be already paying out large amounts of alimony. He was an incorrigible faller-in-love, she thought, half-amused and half-angry. But at least he married the girls. She hoped this one would last.

Charles said, 'I've been trying to persuade her to marry me—she's been staying in London with friends—and when she went back to the US I thought I'd lost her. But last night she phoned me to say yes. I'm over the moon, as you can imagine,' he ended exultantly. 'You'll love Gabrielle; you couldn't help it.'

Josie thought of her mother, whose life had been ruined by this Don Juan. But you couldn't change people. She lifted her glass to him. 'Congratulations,' she said. 'I hope you'll be very happy.'

'Thank you, Jo, I know I will. I've found the right woman at last.' Charles couldn't keep off the subject of Gabrielle long, and the eulogy lasted all through lunch. Josie enjoyed the superbly cooked food, but she doubted if her father knew what he was eating.

But finally he seemed to remember why he had asked her to come. 'A little matter between our two solicitors, Jo, concerning a property in the South of France I bought many years ago. I've always been intending to renovate it and put it on the market, but I've never got around to it. My agents down there have dealt with letting it out to visitors, but now I have a client who is interested in buying it "as is" and I've decided to sell.'

Seeing Josie begin to look a little puzzled, he went on quickly, 'But my solicitor finds that the property is registered in your mother's name, and so will have been transferred to you under her will. Are you with me?'

'I think so,' Josie said. 'What do you want me to do?'

'Briefly, just fix things up with your solicitor and see that the deeds are transferred to my name. I can't think why it was put into your mother's name, but it was bought many years ago. It was probably done to escape some tax or other. Will you do this for me?'

She nodded. 'I'll see Uncle Seb and ask him to clear things up.'

'Thanks a lot, my dear. I'm tidying up various odds and ends just now. If there's any balance due to you my solicitors will see you right.'

He finished his coffee at a gulp. 'Are you ready, Jo? Sorry to rush you. I've got an appointment at three, and I'm off to New York tomorrow, and I have a lot to get through before I leave.'

When she had seen Charles off, Josie phoned Uncle Seb's office and made an appointment to see him when he finished with his last client. That gave her time to stroll down to the big stores in Oxford Street and do some shopping. She'd planned to give herself a couple of weeks' holiday now that she had sold the family house in St John's Wood. She'd go to Cornwall, perhaps; Cornwall would be lovely in June—not too crowded.

She bought three sundresses, and then took a taxi to Uncle Seb's office. 'Uncle Seb' was Sebastian Cross of Cross, French and Abercrombie in Lincoln's Inn Fields. He had been her mother's friend and solicitor for as long as Josie could remember, and was now hers. He had seen her mother through her divorce seven years ago and helped her through the bad time afterwards. Her mother had always relied on him and he had never failed to do all he could for them both.

When Josie was shown into his impressive office he greeted her affectionately and settled her into a comfortable chair opposite him at his big desk.

His shrewd grey eyes smiled at her. 'I was going to phone to ask you to call in and have a chat about your property in France, Josie,' he said, drawing a folder towards him.

'*My* property? It isn't mine; it's my father's. I've just had lunch with him and he asked me to have the deeds transferred into his name and let his solicitors have them.'

Sebastian frowned and drew some papers from the folder. 'I don't get this, Josie. Tell me exactly what he said.'

Josie had a good memory, and she recounted her father's words accurately, adding, 'He said if there was anything due to me his solicitors would see me right.'

Sebastian's lip curled. 'Very generous of him!'

Josie looked worriedly at him. She had always known that Charles and Uncle Seb didn't get on. 'You don't think there's anything wrong, do you? Charles seemed a little mixed up, but I'm sure he wouldn't try to cheat me.'

Sebastian examined the papers before him. After a long pause he lifted his head and said, 'Listen, Josie. I knew both your mother and your father, even before they were married, and I'm not at all mixed up about what happened. I've always handled your mother's affairs, and I dealt with the transaction regarding the house in France on her behalf. Your house is one of two. The original owners had a large villa divided to make two quite separate houses. Soon after your parents were married the houses both came on the market at the same time. Your father wanted to buy them both and put them together again to make one large villa which he could sell at a good price. He bought the larger house, but there wasn't enough in the kitty to buy both. It was early in his career and he didn't want to approach his bank manager to ask for a larger overdraft. About that time your mother had a legacy from a godmother, and she used the money to buy the second, smaller house. I dealt with the purchase for her and the house was, of course, put into her name. It has always belonged to her. So, as you are the sole beneficiary under your mother's will, the house belongs to you. We held the deeds at this office and they are at present away, being transferred into your name. You could, of course, sell the house to your father, but it wouldn't be a little matter of "seeing you right". It must be worth a good deal of money.'

Josie's smooth brow was creased. 'But I don't understand. Why didn't I know about it? Why didn't Mother tell me?'

Sebastian sighed. 'Your mother was no business woman. She left everything of that sort to Charles. She probably never gave the matter another thought—never even knew where the house was.'

Josie had been sitting forward, listening to all this, and now she lay back in her chair. 'So I own a house in France! Marvellous! Where is it, Uncle Seb, and have you seen it?'

He nodded. 'I saw the outside of it a couple of years ago when we were touring the South of France. It's in the hills above Menton, which is a delightful town on the Côte d'Azur, about a mile from the Italian border.'

Josie clapped her hands. 'It sounds heavenly. When can I see it?'

'Any time,' he told her. 'I've been in touch with the agents down there, and they have had instructions to cancel any further lettings. So your house is now vacant. I gather that someone has bought the adjoining property. I hope you'll have decent neighbours.'

'Splendid,' Josie said. 'I'll go down as soon as I can. I can't wait to see my house.'

Sebastian frowned slightly. 'Just a word of warning. I don't know what sort of state you'll find it in, after being let out all these years.'

'I don't care,' Josie told him gaily. 'So long as it has four walls and a roof, I can deal with everything else.'

Sebastian stood up and walked to a cupboard, murmuring about the optimism of youth. He took out a key, which he handed to her together with a note he scribbled on a pad. 'This is the address of the house, Mon Abri, and the address of the agents in Menton.'

Josie stowed the key and the note carefully away in her shoulder bag as she walked to the door.

They stood together at the top of the stairs.

Josie said, 'I'm so thrilled about this, Uncle Seb. It's the nicest thing that has happened to me in years, perhaps the nicest thing ever. Thank you for every-

thing.' She reached up and kissed his cheek. 'I promise to let you know what happens.'

'Yes, do that, Josie. And if you want any help you
know where to find me.'

'I'll remember that,' Josie told him, and with a little
wave she ran down the stairs.

She didn't know, of course, how Sebastian lingered
on the landing, looking down at her, or how his clever
eyes softened as he thought that every time he saw
Josie she grew more lovely, more like her mother at
that age. But Marion had been soft and clinging. Josie
had a kind of gallant independence, with her frank
look and her laughing eyes and the tilt of her head.
She'd had a bad time, caring for her mother and trying
to keep up her design work all these years, and she'd
never had time for the fun that all girls expected. She
deserved a break, and he hoped this new interest
would give her one. She was very young, though, at
twenty-three, to be taking charge of an unknown
house in a foreign country. He hoped that all would
go well with her.

Josie felt as if she was walking on air as she left
Uncle Seb's office. It was very hot and the rush-hour
crowd, fighting its way irritably to bus or tube,
seemed denser than usual, but she hardly noticed
when a large, angular woman jostled her or when a
fat, red-faced man stepped on her foot without apology.

Soon she would be away from all this, away from
the poky two-room flat she was renting in a shabby
old house in Bloomsbury. She would be in her own

home—already she thought of it as home—on the
Côte d'Azur, with the blue Mediterranean below.

When she reached her flat it felt hot and stuffy, and
she opened the window, drew the curtains and made
a pot of tea in the minuscule kitchen. She removed
from the table in the sitting-room the design she'd
been working on when Charles had phoned, put the
tray down and got out a notebook and pencil. Then,
with the excitement of a child planning for a holiday,
she began to make a list, starting: 1. Give month's
notice and pay rent in lieu. 2. Visit bank and find out
about travellers' cheques. 3. Pack up everything and
decide where I can leave it until I send for it. 4.
Choose clothes to take—not more than will go into
hand luggage. And so on until she reached the bottom
of the pad.

Josie sat back to drink her tea. Yes, there was going
to be quite a lot to do, but if she worked hard she
would get through it in a few days. Then—off to
Menton. She hugged herself. A week today she would
be in Menton, breathing the tang of fresh sea air, starting out on a new life. She couldn't wait to begin.

CHAPTER ONE

'WHAT the hell are you doing here? Squatting? *Que faites-vous ici? Allez-vous en—vite!*'

The deep, angry voice sounded to Josie like thunder as it reached her through thick layers of sleep. She hated storms. She reached for the duvet, to pull it over her head. It wasn't there. 'Damn!' she muttered. It must have fallen on the floor again.

She rolled over and put out a hand to the familiar bedside lamp. There was no lamp, no table beside the bed either. She opened her eyes wide in the darkened room.

Then she froze as she saw the huge figure looming up above her, and she knew she was having a nightmare. She tried to scream, but no sound came through her parched lips. The menacing figure did not move. Josie clutched her throat. She was icy cold and shaking all over.

Then at last the figure moved. There was the sound of heavy footsteps on the tiled floor, a creak as the shutters were folded back and a little light came into the room.

Josie pulled herself up. Her brain wasn't working properly yet but she knew that this wasn't a nightmare. There was a man in the room.

Indignation displaced fear. 'How dare you?' she croaked. 'Get out of my room.'

Memory returned in a flash. She had been so tired, so hot after the long journey from London to the South of France, that when she'd found her house, Mon Abri, just behind Menton at last, and opened the front door into what seemed to be a sitting-room, all she'd been able to do was grope her way into the darkened interior, drag off her sundress and collapse on to a divan.

The man walked back and stood looking down at her. Josie was suddenly, sickeningly aware that she was wearing nothing but a lacy bra and minuscule briefs. With a gasp she leaned over the edge of the divan and groped feverishly for the sundress. It was damp and crumpled, and when she held it up in front of her it covered her rather inadequately, from her neck to her thighs.

'Ah, what a pity!' the man said softly, and Josie, now completely awake, felt more scared than she had ever done in her life.

'Get out,' she quavered.

'That's exactly what *you* are going to do. And what do you think you're doing here anyway? Squatting? Or have you been watching my comings and goings and decided to display your—er—attractions?' His arm shot out and he ripped the sundress away from her and dropped it on the floor again. 'You're wasting your time, my girl. I prefer brunettes.'

Josie gave a strangled gasp of fury. If only she could have got to her feet and delivered a hefty blow to whatever part of his body she could reach! But he was standing so close that if she had tried to stand up she would have had to touch him, and she dared not think what might happen then, in spite of his insulting rejection. What sort of a man was he, anyway? She glanced up at him, but he was standing with his back to the window, and, apart from the fact that he was tall and broad and dark, she couldn't make out very much of him. He had an educated voice, but that didn't mean anything.

Before she could think of a suitably cutting retort he was speaking again. 'I don't know why you've parked yourself here, or if you are expecting your young friends to join you,' he said smoothly. 'But, whatever the reason, I suggest that you get some clothes on and take yourself off, pronto. If you're not out of here in ten minutes I'll come back and remove you. I'm living in the next house, so I can watch your departure.'

With a final glance at her near-naked body he turned away and walked quickly out of the room, closing the front door behind him.

Josie swung her legs off the divan and stood up. Her knees felt like india rubber. For a full minute she stared at the closed door, seething with rage.

When Uncle Seb had warned her that she would have neighbours she hadn't given any thought to the matter, but if this horrible man were to be her neighbour it was going to be disastrous. Had he got a family with him or was he here alone? If he was alone she couldn't possibly stay.

Then she clicked her tongue impatiently. What was she thinking of? Her hazel eyes narrowed and her soft mouth hardened into a firm line. She certainly wasn't going to let a pig of a man spoil her pleasure and excitement in taking over her new house on the French Riviera. To have to put up with neighbours at such close quarters was an unwelcome shock, but she told herself that it was just her bad luck that her first encounter with a neighbour should have been so upsetting.

Why had the beastly man been so abominably rude? She couldn't imagine, but there was only one way to find out; confront him and demand an explanation and an apology. She smiled grimly as she pictured just how she would make him grovel.

Lifting her travel bag on to the divan, she rummaged through it and selected a clean sundress. Her hand encounted a packet of tea-bags in the corner of the bag. She pulled it out with a cry of delight. A cup of tea was just what she needed to revive her and boost up her energy to face her insolent neighbour.

Slipping the crisp blue sundress over her head, and running a comb through her russet curls, she surveyed the room for the first time. It was long and L-shaped, and bore all the evidence of summer-letting to visitors. There were two lumpy easy chairs, and a badly scratched dining-table with four dining-chairs in place. A huge sideboard stood against one wall and the divan on which she had been lying was pushed against the opposite wall, which must be the dividing wall between the two houses. There was a staircase leading up to the first floor and a door to the left of it, which would be the kitchen door.

The kitchen, when she had pulled back the shutters to let some light in, proved to be tiny. There was a sink and one tap, a worktop with a kettle on it, two or three cupboards, a few hooks on the wall, and that was all. She would have to change everything, she thought, but meanwhile—tea.

She turned on the tap, but nothing happened except a faint gurgle. The water was evidently turned off. She got on to her knees and tried to find a tap under the sink. There was no tap, but her groping fingers encountered a pipe which seemed to run along the wall and disappear into the next-door house.

Josie's smouldering rage burst into flames. The wretch must have turned off her water supply to make sure she could not stay here. Well, she would see about that.

With the light of battle in her large hazel eyes, she strode out through her front door to the door marked Maison les Roches, which must be the next house. There was no bell, so she knocked hard, which relieved her feelings slightly but bruised her knuckles. When there was no reply she pushed the door. It opened into what was evidently the main sitting-room, which was in better condition than her room next door. There were comfortable chairs, rugs on the floor and an elegant staircase on one side of the room. Its elegance was rather marred by the fact that the wall which divided the two houses seemed to push itself against the carved balusters. A small table with two chairs stood on the opposite side of the room and on it was—wonder of wonders—a steaming teapot, a jug of milk and one cup.

The delicious smell of freshly brewed tea was too much for Josie. Sitting down in one of the chairs, she poured a cup for herself, added milk and drank blissfully. That was better. Now she could give all her attention to defeating the Enemy.

Footsteps sounded above her head, and a moment later the Enemy appeared at the top of the stairs. Josie put down her empty cup and stood up, ready for battle.

The man evidently hadn't seen her yet, and it was her first chance to get a good look at him. The light had been dim next door, but in here there were wall-fittings which lit up the room. He had obviously just had a shower. He wore khaki shorts and nothing else and his dark hair was flattened to his head and dripping on to his shoulders. He padded barefoot down the stairs, took the towel from round his neck and rubbed his hair vigorously.

A quick all-over glance showed Josie a tall, broad-shouldered man, probably in the mid-thirties. She had to admit that he was magnificently built, with the muscular body of an athlete. The towel he was wielding partly covered his face, but she could see his eyes. They were strange eyes, steel-grey with a darker rim round the irises.

He threw down the towel and looked round the room to see her standing beside the table. She met his eyes with a faint apologetic smile. 'I've helped myself to a cup of your tea,' she said. 'I felt that you owed me that. There's plenty left in the pot.'

He ignored her words. He stood quite still, but she saw the steely grey eyes narrow and his hands clench. 'You don't give up, do you?' he said, with the same soft contempt he had used before. 'I thought I told you to clear out.'

'Well, as you can see, I chose not to obey your order.' She tried to sound mocking, but this had no effect on him. 'I came to—'

She had no chance to finish the sentence. In three long strides he had crossed the space between them and a second later she was in his arms.

'Oh, I know why you came.' The grey eyes were only inches from her own alarmed ones, his mouth almost touching hers. 'And if this is what you want you shall have it.' His arms tightened around her and his mouth came down on hers.

He kissed her almost savagely, at the same time drawing her closer still against his hard body.

Josie had been taken completely by surprise, but now she managed to get her wits back. 'No,' she gasped against his mouth, struggling wildly. He was holding her so tightly against him that she couldn't get her hands up between their two bodies.

The kiss went on and on. She kept her lips tightly closed but he forced them open. She had never been kissed like this before, never so intimately, and suddenly her body responded with a mad need to take part in this crazy emotion of anger, or lust, or whatever it was. She wanted to press herself against him, to kiss him back as intimately as he was kissing her, to dig her nails into his smooth, warm back. A few moments of weakness possessed her, and she thought she was going to faint.

Then he lifted his head and held her a little away from him. 'Maybe I don't prefer brunettes after all,' he said softly, and would have drawn her back to him, but Josie saw her opportunity at last. She gathered all

her strength to push him away and delivered a sting-
ing blow to his cheek.

He backed off, one hand to his face. He was
breathing as fast as she was, and Josie tried to think
of her plan to make him grovel but nothing occurred
to her.

He said in angry exasperation, 'What do you want
here, then?'

Her knees were shaking and her throat was tight
but she managed to say, with what dignity she could
muster, 'I came to ask you to turn on the water supply
to my kitchen.' She remembered that that was the first
sentence in her grovel routine. Then he was meant to
say, in surprise, *Your* kitchen? and she would take it
from there.

To her surprise, he laughed. 'Well, that's a wonderful anticlimax. Now let's have the truth—all of it.
How did you manage to get in next door when it was
locked up?'

He had missed his cue, but this would do as well—
better, really. 'I had a key to my own house, of
course,' Josie said loftily. Her hand encountered a
chair behind her and she sat down on it rather quickly.
The compelling eyes, fixed so relentlessly on her,
were making her feel unnerved.

She said shakily, 'I'm very tired. If you will please
turn on the water I'll go back and have a night's
sleep.' She passed her hand wearily across her eyes.

He stood still, looking down at her darkly. Then he
walked across the room and opened a door. When he
came back he said, 'I've turned the water on. I suppose I can't throw you out tonight. But you'll have

to go first thing tomorrow morning. I don't want squatters here.'

She braced her knees and walked to the door. She turned as she opened it. 'I think you're detestable,' she said.

Outside it was quite dark. The sky was thick with stars, and the only sound was the constant loud chirping of the cicadas. That sound triggered the memory of a holiday in the little seaside resort of Boulouris, near Saint Raphael, with both her parents when she was about ten. Her mother had been so happy then. Josie didn't want to think about what had happened afterwards.

She found her own front door, and, once inside, felt round for a light switch, making a mental note that she must buy a good strong torch. At last her fingers encountered the switch. She turned it on and was rewarded by a feeble light from an unshaded central hanging fitting, which was just enough to allow her to find her way across the room.

The tiny kitchen was even more inadequately lit, but she found the tap and turned it on. The water spurted out with such force that it splashed up from the sink and soaked the front of her dress. She muttered all the bad words she knew about the Enemy next door. It was all his fault. Oh, well, the dress would soon dry in the heat of the house. It was unbearably hot, and Josie wondered if she should keep the window in the sitting-room open to let in the cool evening air. But she decided not to risk insect bites.

Upstairs, she groped around both bedrooms to find

switches, none of which yielded any light. She would have to sleep on the divan in the room below.

Downstairs in the kitchen again, Josie yawned hugely. What she really needed was sleep, but first she must eat something. She had bought some provisions in Menton, when the bus from Nice Airport had set her down there, and now she opened the plastic carrier and found a baguette, some butter, which had melted all over the bag, and a packet of cheese.

There were three mugs in one of the cupboards, and she chose the best of these, rinsed it and filled it with water. She pulled off hunks of bread and broke pieces of cheese from the packet. Her first dinner in her new house! She chuckled, refusing to feel disappointed. Everything could be put right, given time—and money. She wouldn't think about the horrible man next door. He would leave her alone when he realised that she was really the owner of Mon Abri.

When she had finished all she could manage to eat, she refilled the mug and took it back to the sitting-room. She carried a small chair to the divan, to act as a bedside table, and on this she set the mug of water, her watch and a silver-framed snapshot of her mother, taken in the garden of their house last year. She picked it up and looked into the wan, lined face which had once been beautiful. 'This is my new house, Mum dear. You should have come with me,' Josie whispered, her eyes suddenly misty with tears. 'But I don't think you would have cared for it very much. Certainly not as it is at present.'

Marion Dunn had liked everything neat and predictable, and when, eight years ago, her husband left her for a younger woman the shock had been too much for her. She had gone to pieces. When she'd received the final divorce papers she had collapsed. 'My life is over,' she had mourned. And sometimes Josie thought that was true. Every year her mother had suffered from some new ailment, and when a bad attack of flu had struck her last winter she had not had the strength to resist. She had developed pneumonia, and in spite of all Josie's care had died six months ago, just after Christmas.

Josie put the photograph down again on the chair. She had loved her mother sincerely, and she missed her, but the years had shown her what resentment and self-pity could do to a woman if she gave way to them. Her mother had been so romantic, but women were more realistic now, the twenty-three-year-old Josie told herself confidently. They didn't break their hearts over men.

It would be lovely to have a shower and wash off all the hot stickiness of the day, but the shower-room, like the other two rooms upstairs, was in darkness. She pulled off her clothes, draped the sundress over a chair to dry and left her bra and lacy pants on the floor, to be washed tomorrow when she had found out how to get hot water. Fortunately there was a tiny cloakroom beside the front door, and she washed her face and wiped wet hands over her hot body, drying herself with the small hand towel she had brought with her to use on the journey. She found a thin nightie in her bag and put it on, covering her body quickly.

Suddenly her cheeks flamed as she remembered

that kiss. It had been a warning to her that her body could betray her so shamefully. But the Enemy was clearly a past master in the art of—she had been going to say 'lovemaking', but of course it had nothing to do with love. She must forget all about it.

She yawned. She would leave the centre light on; she wouldn't feel quite safe in the dark. There was no bedcover, but she wouldn't need it. She took a light gown from her bag and tucked it under the cushion that would serve as a pillow, in case it got cool in the night. Then, with a deep sigh, she stretched out on the divan. She'd have a lovely, undisturbed sleep.

She had expected to drop off to sleep immediately, but instead she found herself wondering what she was going to say to the Enemy next-door when she saw him in the morning. He didn't believe that she owned the house. It was quite ridiculous that she had to convince him, but somehow she must do so. She remembered the strength of his arms when he held her, and felt again the weakness in her limbs. Oh, yes, if he chose to be nasty he could well evict her bodily, as he had threatened to do.

She had no actual proof of ownership, but she must be absolutely sure of it in her own mind. She had taken Uncle Seb's word for it, but what if there had been some mistake? No, there couldn't be. Uncle Seb couldn't possibly be wrong. She would rely on him and ask for his help if she needed it. She wouldn't be bullied by that hateful man next door. Mon Abri was hers, and she meant to keep it.

Closing her eyes on this firm resolution, she fell into a heavy sleep.

CHAPTER TWO

JOSIE'S hope for an undisturbed sleep was not realised. In the middle of the night she awoke with a start. Something cold and wet had crawled across her face. She sat up, her heart thumping. A snake? A lizard? With a cry of horror she made herself lift a shaking hand to brush it away, but her fingers encountered only water, and at the same moment a larger splash fell on her back and trickled coldly down her spine. More large splashes followed. She was wide awake now, and swung herself off the divan. Looking up, she saw that the ceiling had an ominous crack in it. At that moment the crack opened further, and the water that had been gathering behind poured down, straight on to the divan.

Josie grabbed her gown, but it was soaking. She lifted her bag, the photograph and her watch on to the table and pushed it to the other side of the room. They all seemed to have escaped the deluge up to now. She squinted at her watch and saw that it was twenty past two. There was only one urgent thought in her mind now—the water had to be turned off and the tap was in the next-door house.

Rummaging in her bag, she found an old pair of jeans she had brought with her for work in the garden. She pulled them on over her nightie and raced along the path to the next house. There was no reply to her loud banging, but she found that again the door wasn't locked. She went in and felt around for a switch. The room was flooded with light. She yelled several times at the top of her voice 'Help! Is anyone there?' No reply. Josie looked uncertainly up the stairs. The man must be sleeping the sleep of the dead. Well, he was going to be rudely awakened.

At the top of the stairs there was a landing with four doors. One was partly open to disclose a bathroom. She banged on the other three doors in turn, shouting, 'Help! Emergency!'

Still no response.

She looked doubtfully at the three doors. She had to find the man, and fast. Choosing the middle door, she opened it and snapped on the light. She'd been lucky in choosing the right room, but only at this moment did she wonder if the man was here alone. She saw with relief that the hump in the bed belonged to one body only. His face was half-buried in the pillow, and a lock of dark hair fell across his forehead. There was a sheet covering the lower half of his body but the top half was naked. Josie hoped he was wearing pyjama trousers, but this was no time for maidenly modesty. She walked across the room and grabbed his shoulder with both hands, shaking it as hard as she could. His skin felt warm and slightly moist under her fingers, and the muscles stiffened in resistance to pressure. At last he opened his eyes and blinked up at her in the light.

'What the devil…?' he muttered.

'Wake up!' she shouted. 'Go down and turn the water off—now—or we'll be flooded out.'

He blinked again, and focused on her face. *'You!'* he growled. 'Look here, I've had just about enough of—'

She gave him another shake. 'Never mind what you've had enough of. Come down and turn the water off or we'll both be drowned.' She didn't know whether the crack in the ceiling would reach to both houses, but that didn't matter. It was her own house that was suffering at the moment.

He levered himself up in the bed. 'What?' he shouted angrily.

Josie gathered all her patience. 'Flood,' she said, slowly and clearly. 'Water. Coming through the ceiling. Come down and turn the tap off.'

She seemed to have got through to him at last. He threw back the sheet and got out of bed. Josie was relieved to see that he *was* wearing pyjama trousers. Cursing under his breath, he stumbled down the stairs and into the kitchen. Josie followed and waited for him at the bottom of the stairs. When he came out of the kitchen he glared at her and said nastily, 'Well, I've turned off your water. What sort of game are you playing? First you want the water on, then you want it off. Is it your idea of a joke?' He evidently hadn't taken in all she had told him.

'You'd better come and look,' she said, turning towards the door.

He stood where he was. He obviously wasn't a man who liked to be given orders. But as she reached her sitting-room Josie heard his bare feet padding along behind her.

Inside, the tiled floor was awash. Thank goodness

she'd put her bag and the other things out of harm's way on the table.

The man was close behind her. 'What happened, exactly?' he said irritably, just as if she was responsible. 'What were you doing to cause this?'

'Don't be idiotic.' Josie had completely lost her temper with him. 'Look up there,' she added dramatically, pointing to the widening crack in the ceiling.

He looked up, frowning darkly. Then he splashed across the floor and examined the crack. Water had stopped pouring and was now merely dripping. He pulled the divan out of the line of fire and turned back to her. 'How did you find out what was happening down here?' he asked.

Josie said, 'I was sleeping on the divan and I was dripped on.'

'Why on the divan? What's wrong with the bedrooms?'

She sighed heavily. 'Do I have to go through this third degree? Briefly, none of the rooms upstairs has lights. The bulbs must have expired. I don't happen to carry a storm lantern round with me.'

Without another word he ran up the stairs and was down again in about half a minute. 'You're right,' he said, joining her at the table. And then, wearily, 'Well, you'll have to finish your night's sleep in one of my spare rooms.'

'No,' Josie snapped.

'Now who's being idiotic?' the man said. 'You can't sleep here.'

'Of course I can. I can feel my way into one of the beds upstairs. Or perhaps you could lend me a torch?'

He picked up her bag. 'No,' she squealed, hastily pushing the silver-framed photograph into it and slipping the bracelet of the watch on to her wrist.

'Yes,' he said. 'Come along.' He put a hand on her back to urge her to the door. 'Good Lord, you're soaking wet, girl.'

Josie hadn't had time to find a sweater before she rushed for help. Now she realised that the top of her thin nightie must have taken most of the first drips of water before she escaped. She also realised that his hand was still spread out on her back. She tried to twist away, but he was pushing her relentlessly to the door.

'I'll be OK,' she muttered.

He ignored that. 'Everything can wait until morning,' he said, and now he sounded very tired. 'I want the rest of my sleep even if you don't. No, don't argue. I've no intention of pouncing on you; you needn't worry about that.'

She shrugged and gave in. He was much too strong to fight with.

In the next house he led her upstairs and into one of the bedrooms. Switching on the light, he said, 'There you are,' and yawned. 'Now, find something dry to put on and get into bed. I'll bring you a cup of tea. You look as if you need it.'

His eyes passed dismissively over her as she stood, shivering, in the middle of the room, her hair lank and the thin nightie clinging revealingly to the top part of her body. She must look a sight, but it wasn't kind of him to remind her of it. 'Don't make tea specially for me,' she said, biting her lip to stop her teeth chattering.

'Of course not,' he said, and went out of the room.

Josie pulled off the jeans and the damp nightie and found another nightie in her bag, one that wasn't at all revealing. Slipping it over her head, she went along to the bathroom next door. She looked longingly at the modern shower, but that would have to wait until the morning. So she washed her face and hands and towelled her hair. Then she returned to the bedroom.

She was too tired to take in any details of the room, but the rugs were soft and the double bed was blissfully comfortable as she crawled into it and propped herself up against the pillows. She was looking forward to the cup of tea, however ungraciously it had been offered.

A few minutes later there was a tap at the door and the man appeared, bearing a mug, which he put down on the bedside table.

'Thank you,' Josie said, 'And thank you for taking charge of things. You've been kind.'

His lips turned down. 'Enlightened self-interest, it's called,' he said enigmatically. He switched on the bedside lamp. 'Don't you want your photograph beside you? I saw you pushing it away lovingly into your bag.'

She almost laughed. He must imagine that the photograph was of some boyfriend—or even a husband. She shrugged. 'It doesn't matter,' she said. And let him make what he could of that.

He looked rather hard at her, but didn't press the

point. 'There's a lock on the door,' he said, 'and by the way, what's your name?'

'Josie,' she said. 'What's yours?'

For a moment she thought he wasn't going to reply. Then he said, 'Leon.' He walked across the room, switched off the light and opened the door. Then without another word he went out of the room and closed the door firmly behind him.

A charming host! Josie thought with a grin, but at least he had brought her some tea.

She sat up in bed and sipped it, relishing the feeling of the hot liquid slipping down her throat and spreading heat through her whole body. She hadn't known she was so cold.

She finished the tea, put the mug on the table, switched off the bedside lamp and snuggled down into the soft bed.

After the hard lumpiness of the divan it felt heavenly. This time she was sure she would sleep undisturbed, and she didn't bother to get up to lock the door. She pulled the light duvet up to her chin, yawned luxuriously and was asleep almost immediately.

Josie had her uninterrupted sleep at last. She woke to see sunlight making bright thin lines along the shutters. When she consulted her watch she saw that it was half-past seven. Getting out of bed, she crossed the room and opened the door a crack. The next door was wide open, and from below came the sounds of a man in the kitchen—various thumps and clatters. Her gown had suffered the fate of the divan, but the bathroom was only next door so she grabbed a pair of shorts and a white top and sprinted along the passage. She decided against a shower, just had a quick wash, and had just got into her clothes when there was an enormous crash from below followed by loud expletives. She smiled to herself, and had started to dry her hair when there was a loud banging on the door and Leon's voice saying, 'May I come in? I need a bottle of antiseptic from the cupboard.'

Josie heard the urgency in his voice and, pushing back her damp curls, opened the door. Leon was wearing jeans cut off at the knee. The rest of him was bare and his left hand was covered in blood. He grunted his thanks and began to rummage awkwardly in the wall cupboard with his right hand.

Josie had taken a course in first aid when she was looking after her mother, and she took charge immediately. 'Put your hand under the cold tap,' she instructed in her best ward-sister's tone. 'I'll find the antiseptic.'

He did as he was told with surprising meekness, holding on to the side of the bowl with his other hand. 'Bread knife,' he explained weakly. He looked very pale.

Josie found a bottle of iodine and a new roll of bandages in the cupboard, and, lifting his forearm by the elbow, saw that a deep gash down the side of his hand was bleeding freely. She cut off a length of bandage with the scissors provided and made it into a thick pad, which she pressed firmly over the wound, glancing again at his face. She saw that he was paler still.

'I'm sorry,' he said weakly. 'I'm OK.' He swayed on his feet as he spoke.

Josie pulled the bathroom stool behind him, still holding on to the pad. 'Sit down and get your head between your knees. Lower than that.' She pushed his head down further. How thick and crisp his dark hair was under her fingers, she thought, letting her hand remain on his neck. His skin was bronzed, except for a paler line where his hair had been clipped at the nape. She had a mad urge to lean down and put her lips against it. She stood up quickly, trembling inside. The sheer physical magnetism of the man was dangerous. She must be very careful or she might make a fool of herself. She cringed as she remembered his look of cynical contempt when he'd thought she was trying to seduce him. That had been a misunderstanding, but it had shown, only too plainly, what he thought of an unwanted advance from her sex.

After a few minutes he sat up, and she was pleased to see the colour coming back into his face. Very carefully she lifted a corner of the pad. 'Oh, good,' she said cheerfully. 'The bleeding has almost stopped. I'll put some iodine on, so hold your breath.'

He didn't even wince when she applied the antiseptic, although it must have stung horribly. She found lint to cover the wound and then bandaged the hand firmly. 'There you are,' she said with satisfaction. 'You mustn't use your left hand much or you'll become a hospital case if the bleeding starts again.'

He looked up at her as she cleaned the wash-basin and tidied the cupboard. 'You're very professional,' he said. 'Are you a nurse?'

She shook her head, putting the scissors back in their case. 'No, but I looked after my mother, who was a semi-invalid and always having accidents of one sort or another. She died some months ago.'

'I'm sorry,' he said quietly. 'But I appreciate your expertise. I make a fool of myself where my own blood is concerned, but I don't seem to react to other people's blood. There's a question for a psychiatrist.'

Josie smiled. 'We'd better not go into that. Now, come down when you feel like it and I'll see what I can do with the bread knife.'

In her bedroom, Josie put on sandals and ran a comb through her curls. She was smiling as she ran downstairs. She seemed to have formed some sort of understanding with the man, and that would make things much more pleasant if they were to be neighbours.

The kitchen was large and modern, nothing like her poor affair next door. She was suddenly aware that she hadn't given a thought to the chaos in Mon Abri since last night, but that would have to wait.

Leon had evidently been trying to cut a stale baguette into slices for toast, using a plate instead of a wooden board. Naturally, the bread had slipped on the plate, which was now lying in fragments on the floor. 'Men!' she muttered.

She found a brush in the cupboard and brushed up the pieces of broken plate, then carefully washed the bread knife. Then she cut more slices of baguette, which she put in the wide-mouthed toaster. She made one cup of instant coffee and set the small round table with one plate and knife, butter from the fridge and three different kinds of jam.

As she was taking out the toast Leon appeared in the doorway. In spite of his injured hand he had managed to dress neatly in jeans and a cream silk shirt. His springy dark hair was brushed tidily. He really was very good-looking, Josie thought. She said, 'I've made some toast. Was that what you were trying to do?'

He nodded and sat down at the table. 'Are you going to join me?'

'Yes, if I'm invited,' Josie said.

'The least I can do,' he said. 'Please sit down and join me for breakfast.'

She put an extra knife and plate on the table, made a mug of coffee, and sat down opposite him. She found that she was extremely hungry, and munched toast and apricot jam ravenously. She glanced apologetically at Leon, who was having some difficulty because of his tightly bandaged hand. She knew better than to offer to cut up the toast for him. He wasn't the kind of man who would tolerate nannying. 'Sorry I'm being a pig,' she said. 'I can't remember when I had a proper meal.'

'Carry on,' he said, sitting back in his chair and eyeing her thoughtfully. 'Where did you come from yesterday?' he said.

'From London,' Josie said. 'I bought some basic food in Menton, before I took a taxi up here, but by the time I'd found my house I was too hot and tired to eat, so I just flopped down on the nearest flat surface.' She pulled a face and added, 'Until you disturbed me so ungallantly.' She laughed lightly. If they could share a joke that would put the embarrassing incident in its true perspective.

But there was no laughter, not even a smile in the strange grey eyes as he regarded her narrowly. 'What gives you the idea that Mon Abri belongs to you?' he enquired.

Josie choked on a piece of toast. She had begun to like this man, to think that he liked her, that they would be able to talk together rationally. But his tone and the way he had framed his question made it an insult.

'I resent that. I certainly own Mon Abri. What right have you to question it?' She spoke calmly, but danger signals flashed in the hazel-green eyes.

He frowned, puzzled. 'How old are you, Josie?'

She kept her temper with an effort. 'I really don't see what my age has to do with the matter, but, if you must know, I'm twenty-three.'

He stared at her, dark brows raised. 'Well, well, I was a long way out. When I first saw you, stretched out on the divan, I took you for about fifteen—one of a party of youngsters who were wandering about the world. I expected to see your friends joining you, setting up a squat in this pleasant place. Then, when you walked into my house and drank my tea, and smiled seductively at me—'

'I didn't smile seductively,' Josie broke in furiously.

'And smiled seductively at me,' he went on, as if she hadn't spoken, 'I upgraded you to a higher age group—say seventeen or eighteen at the most. Yes,

yes—' he held up a hand as she opened her mouth to speak again '—I'm aware that I was mistaken about your intentions. But I don't think I can be blamed for that. I must say I thought again when you saved me from bleeding to death just now, but twenty-three! No, I shouldn't have guessed that. It makes a difference.'

Josie gritted her teeth. 'I suppose I may be allowed to own a house at twenty-three?'

'Certainly. But not the house next door. And in case you're going to say why not, it's because I shall own it myself in a few days. I plan to restore the villa to its former glory, to take down the dividing walls and re-plan the rooms.'

'Really?' Josie raised delicate brows. He was so confident, so disgustingly sure of himself, that it would be a pleasure to take him down a peg or two. But she mustn't rush it. 'More coffee?'

'Please.' He pushed his mug across the table. He was not looking at her now. He was staring out of the window. No doubt planning what he was going to do with her house when he obtained it. He had a surprise coming to him, Josie thought, grinning to herself.

He pushed back his chair jerkily and got to his feet. 'Let's go outside and talk this over. Open air clears the head.'

'Are you implying that my head needs clearing?' she demanded acidly.

'Don't be silly.' He grasped her arm and yanked her to her feet unceremoniously. 'Bring the coffee and we'll sit on the terrace.'

Josie had already discovered that he was a man who

got his own way, by superior strength if necessary, and that it was a waste of time to argue. She shook off his hand. The touch of his fingers on her bare arm disturbed her. Oh, dear, if she had to battle with a man in the way of business, why couldn't he have been as lacking in sex appeal to her as were the other men who had appeared in her life from time to time. Except Roger Ward, of course, and he had been married. She filled the two mugs again and followed Leon outside.

There was a white-painted table and chairs at the end of the terrace, where tendrils of vine hung down, making a kind of arbour. Josie thought she must get a similar table for her own end of the terrace.

Leon held out a chair for her politely and took the other one himself. 'This is better. Now, let's get things straight. My name is Kent—Leon Kent, practising architect. You seem to think you own the house next door. I am convinced that I am on the verge of becoming owner myself.' His expression changed. There was no amusement in the strange grey eyes now. His mouth was hard as he added, almost under his breath, 'And I mean to have it.'

Josie stared at him, and a wriggle of fear twisted in her stomach. She was going to have a fight on her hands, for she certainly wasn't going to be bullied into parting with her house, not on any terms.

'Why do you want the house anyway?' he went on. 'What do you propose to do with it?'

'Live in it.'

'Just as it is?'

'Of course not. I intend to refurbish it to my own designs.'

'You're an interior designer?'

'That's what I want to be.'

He looked back at her, and his tone was reasonable now as he said, 'Will you explain your claim to the house?'

Stormy hazel-green eyes looked straight into his. 'I don't have to answer that question. But as it's such a simple answer I'll tell you. It was left to me in my mother's will. If you don't believe me you can have it confirmed by my solicitor, Sebastian Cross of Lincoln's Inn Fields. I have his phone number. Satisfied?' she added defiantly.

He had been frowning as he listened. Now his frown deepened. 'I must get in touch with my own solicitor before I answer that question,' he said. 'There's something very funny going on and I mean to get to the bottom of it.'

Josie thought of her conversation with Uncle Seb and remembered uncomfortably that she, too, had wondered if there had been some mistake. She said, 'May I ask the name of the person who promised to sell the house to you? Was it by any chance Charles Dunn?'

Dark brows rose. 'Yes, it was, although I can't imagine how you could have guessed. He's an old colleague; I've worked with him for some time. You're not suggesting that he has been conning me to get a better price for the house?'

'Certainly not,' Josie said indignantly. 'Charles would never knowingly let a friend down.'

There was a silence, and his eyes narrowed as they watched her face. Then he said, his eyes still on her face, 'You seem to know him very well.'

'I should,' Josie said. 'He's my father.'

Leon's dark brows shot up. His eyes opened wide. She saw that she had really amazed him. Then, with a hint of suspicion in his voice, he asked, 'Why didn't I know you before, then, when I visited Charles at his home?'

She was tempted to throw her coffee cup at him. 'Are you accusing me of being a liar?' She was shaking with rage.

'Calm down, Josie. I was merely asking a reasonable question. You needn't answer if you don't want to.'

She drew in a long breath. The beastly man. He always won an argument. She said, in what she hoped was a dignified voice, 'I seldom see my father these days, although we get along very well when one or other of my stepmothers is out of the way.' Her lips curled expressively.

'I see,' Leon said slowly. 'When you told me your mother had died recently, I thought...' He left the words in the air.

Josie shook her head. 'Oh, no, my parents were divorced years ago. Charles has married and divorced again twice since then.' She smiled tolerantly. 'One side of Charles is a born romantic, always seeking the right woman, although the other side is a keen business man.'

'Well, I hope he was in his business mode when he sold me Mon Abri, but I'll have to have some further information. There must have been some slip-up somewhere.' He got to his feet. 'I'll go and phone my solicitors now, and then we shall know for sure which of us is the owner of the house.'

As Josie began to stand up he said, 'No, don't go away. This concerns both of us.'

He went into the sitting-room through the open French window and Josie listened to him dialling, her hands clenched tightly together.

If he came back and insisted that he was right and she was wrong, she would— What *would* she do?

CHAPTER THREE

THE call to London seemed to take a long time, and
Leon's side of it consisted mainly of, 'Yes,' and, 'No,
I see,' and 'Yes, I understand.' But finally he said
goodbye, and Josie heard the click of the receiver being replaced. There was a long silence after that, until
she felt like screaming. But at last he came back on
to the terrace and sank into his chair.

'Well?' she asked impatiently.

'Not very satisfactory,' he said. 'The three lots of
solicitors are all trying to trace what happened about
twenty years ago, and it seems that until Charles
comes back there is no way they can finalise anything.
He is not expected for several more days, and apparently he's gone to ground in America and can't be
contacted. So,' he said, summing up, 'it seems that
we have to wait until he arrives.' He hesitated. 'I've
been thinking—how would you like to move to a hotel until things are straightened out? Mon Abri isn't
fit to live in at present.'

'I shouldn't like it at all,' Josie said flatly.

He nodded. 'Somehow I didn't think you would.
Well, here's another idea. I took a fortnight off to
come down here and get my builders started, but I'm
happy to treat this next week as a holiday. How about
you? Shall we call off the fight about Mon Abri for
a week? I intend to make contingency plans for put-

ting the two houses together again. You can help me with ideas, and you might also amuse yourself by thinking up schemes for interior decoration. It might be a waste of effort, if my plans come to nothing, but at least it would be good practice for you. What do you think?'

Josie was torn between making an angry refusal and a sneaking feeling that what he suggested would be rather wonderful. And he was right. It would be good practice for her to have the opportunity of watching a top architect at work. She smiled to herself. It was funny how you could always find arguments for doing what you wanted to do.

'Well?' Leon was watching her from lowered lids.

She sighed. 'I suppose if I don't want to be awkward I'd better agree. But it doesn't mean that I give up my claim to Mon Abri,' she added.

He said piously, 'Oh, I'm sure it doesn't. Neither do I give up the expectation that it will soon be mine.'

She looked at him curiously. 'Why are you so keen to get it? Are you going to lose a fat fee from a rich client if you don't?' Perhaps he wanted to bring his wife and family here. Surely he would tell her if that were so.

He shook his head. 'No, no rich client involved.'

'You want it for yourself, then, not professionally?' She looked away, holding her breath.

She was remembering a time at college, when she had fallen passionately in love with Roger Ward, one of the lecturers. It had never amounted to much on his side—merely an occasional lunch and a kiss that thrilled her when he gave her a lift home in his car—

but when he told her he was leaving at the end of term—the next week—she had had wild hopes that he would write to her and ask her to meet him. Then she had heard on the grapevine that he was married, and she had suffered all the agony of heartbreak, although she had had to realise in the end that she had built it all up from her own dreams. But the pain had been real enough, and she wouldn't like to repeat the experience. And now she had to commit herself to spending the next week in the company of a man who had already stirred feelings that were certainly not made up from foolish dreams.

Leon answered her question. 'Well, for my family.'

His family! No explicit mention of a wife. But she had to know. 'Are you married?' she said.

'Married! Good Lord, no. My numerous family is quite enough to cope with, without a wife to complicate things.'

She felt a curious lightness, and a laugh bubbled up as she said, 'I see. So that's why you want a large house?'

'Exactly,' he said, but there was no answering laugh, not even a smile. He wasn't going to talk about his family but that didn't matter. Her most important fear had been laid to rest.

'As a matter of fact, I know both houses quite well. I stayed here some years ago. There was an English family living here then. Delightful people called Martin. I sprained my ankle walking up in the hills near Gorbio, just the other side of Menton. They found me and very kindly brought me back here and looked after me for a couple of weeks. They had a small daughter of about eight or nine, and a married son living in Mon Abri. I saw them often during my holidays here, but we lost touch about eight years ago. I must try to find out where they are and if they are still in France.

'So you see,' Leon went on, 'when Charles told me he was selling the two houses I knew it was just what I'd been looking for and began to plan how I would put them together. Perhaps you may forgive me for greeting you with—er—rather less than courtesy at our first meeting.' He gave Josie a hopeful smile.

She made no response and turned her head away from him. She hadn't forgiven him yet; it was something she needed to remember as a sort of armour against him now he was choosing to show her a different side of his character.

'No? Well, never mind, we'll put all that behind us and be friends for just one week. Friends for a week, Josie?'

His grip was strong, and he held her hand much longer than was necessary. 'Good,' he said warmly. She wished she could believe that he liked her, which was what his smile told her. But she had to be careful. She looked into his grey eyes and reminded herself that they could change to narrow steel blades that could cut with sarcasm or bitter contempt.

Leon stood up. 'If you're going to stay in Mon Abri it will need some attention,' he said. 'Let's go and have a look at it.' He took her hand and they walked across the terrace together. Inside the sitting-room, he stared at the crack in the ceiling. 'It might merely be a faulty joint,' he said. 'If so, I could probably fix it myself. There's a ladder in the outhouse next door; I'll go and fetch it.'

Josie's heart missed a beat as she had a horrible vision of Leon falling and lying senseless beside her. She put a restraining hand on his arm. 'Oh, no, you won't,' she said firmly. 'I refuse to let you climb a ladder and open up that wound in your hand again. It's "enlightened self-interest", to use your own words. What would happen if you "came over all peculiar" at the top of the ladder? I can deal with a cut hand but not a broken leg.'

He clicked his tongue. 'I'll be OK. You said it had stopped bleeding.' He set off again.

'Leon!'

Something in her voice stopped him.

'What?'

'I'm serious,' she said.

He came back towards her. 'Yes, I see you are,' he said slowly. 'OK, Nurse, you win—this time. I'll just take a look upstairs, then. I wonder what condition the bedrooms are in.' He ran lightly up the stairs. When he came back his face was expressionless. 'You'd better go and look for yourself,' he said. 'Meanwhile, I'll go down to Menton and get a plumber up here straight away. I know where to find one. He'll probably know of a cleaner too. Don't say I mustn't drive because of my poor injured hand. My car is automatic. No left hand required. And when I'm down in the town I'll lay in some provisions. We can have our meals together while I'm unable to do the cooking.' He held up his bandaged hand with a pathetic sigh.

'Very clever,' Josie said with a grin.

He returned the grin complacently. 'Well, come and see me off and you can tell me what food you like to cook.'

She walked beside him, itemising chicken and seafood, vegetables and fruit while Leon made a list in his notebook. 'And don't forget the electric bulbs for the upstairs lights.'

He wrote 'Bulbs' and underlined it. At the side of the house was a wide parking space for two or three cars, and Leon's car stood here, a low-slung black convertible.

'Nice car,' Josie said.

He patted the dusty bonnet lovingly. 'Needs a clean. It's a long hop from London.'

She expressed surprise and admiration that he had driven all those miles in one day, and he gave the credit to his car and the excellent French motorways. 'All the same, it's nice to have a compliment from you. Quite a change.'

He unlocked the driver's door and turned to look up at the villa thoughtfully, taking in its lines and proportions as an architect would, Josie thought. 'It's an attractive place,' he said. 'An awful shame that it was carved up.'

Josie looked up at the white house with its pink roof, guarded by clumps of dark pines. If she had no interest in the matter herself she would have had to admit that she agreed with him. But she made no reply, and saw his mouth quirk in amused understanding as he got into the car and wound down the window.

'I'll report on any success with a plumber and cleaner when I get back,' he said. 'See you.'

He reversed the long car skilfully, and drove up the steep driveway, lifting his hand—the bandaged one—in salute.

Josie watched the car disappear through the open gates at the end of the drive and round the bend into the winding road which led down into the town. As she walked slowly back to the villa she found that she was smiling, and that she felt more alive than she had done for months. If she and Leon had to battle over the possession of Mon Abri, it would be better not to be too intense about it.

Yesterday, when she'd arrived by taxi from Menton, Josie hadn't taken in much of the front of the house. All she had wanted was to find Mon Abri and have a long rest. Now, looking around, she saw that the path to the two front doors was fringed on either side with sprawling overgrown bushes which might once have flowered. It all looked wild and untended, but now she was here to care for it, she thought with delight. The bonus was a tall palm tree on her side of the house, and this made her feel that she was indeed on the Mediterranean. She really *must* go down to Menton soon, and see it for herself. But meanwhile there was work to be done.

She decided to explore the remainder of her house, and most certainly she would prepare a bedroom that she could sleep in tonight. Inside the house again, she marched resolutely upstairs, concentrating on the details of her new domain and putting Leon Kent out of her mind.

There appeared to be two bedrooms, as well as the shower-room and a built-in cupboard holding linen and blankets. She would investigate the cupboard later. Meanwhile she looked into the shower-room and decided straight away that it would need completely refitting. She went into the first bedroom.

Leon had evidently opened the long window and folded back the shutters to let in the morning light. She looked around and couldn't help her heart sinking. The room was fairly large, but scantily furnished, with a double bed, small wardrobe, chest of drawers and one upright chair. There was a wooden-framed mirror on the chest, hinged to swing backwards and forwards, with a drawer below. The wooden floor was bare of rugs. Covering everything there was a thick layer of dust. Josie frowned. She had understood from Uncle Seb that the house had been let to visitors, but no visitor had inhabited this room for some time.

Perhaps the other bedroom would be in better condition. It might have been used more recently.

But it looked, if anything, more forlorn. The room was much smaller, probably a child's room. The single bed had been stripped and covered with a grey blanket. There was a wardrobe with drawers inside, and one chair. Here again dust was thick on everything.

Through the open window she saw that there was a narrow iron balcony linking the two bedrooms, and, after testing the safety of it, Josie stepped out. Resting her hands on the rail, she looked down.

Beneath her, the view was quite breathtaking. The Mediterranean almost at her feet! The bedrooms faced the back of the house, but here she was high enough to see what she had not been able to see from the terrace immediately below—a deep blue swathe of sea in the distance and what seemed like hundreds of tiny yachts catching the sun as they bobbled at anchor. Before she'd left London she had provided herself with a guide book to this part of France, and she realised that this must be the famous Menton marina, where luxury yachts from all over the world were moored. Between the house and the sea she looked down over a steeply terraced hillside, with whitewashed villas nestling in clumps of trees, and here and there the startling turquoise of a swimming pool. She could see the road zig-zagging down between the villas until it reached the broad boulevard lined with palm trees which ran along the sea front. Beyond that, nothing but the sparkling blue of sea and the azure blue of sky.

The heat of the day had not yet become intense, and Josie stood, drinking in the view, while the breeze caressed her cheeks and lifted her curls. Stretching her arms wide, she closed her eyes and breathed in the pure air, with its aromatic scent of pine.

Oh, this was a lovely place. She must keep her house, in spite of all its drawbacks, in spite of the fact that Leon Kent quite obviously would like her to give it up—perhaps sell it to him, if he was convinced that she owned it. No, he shouldn't have it. It was hers. Her mouth softened into a wry grin. Her poor little house. Nobody had cared for it. But she was going to change all that, she vowed, as she turned back into the dusty bedroom.

Mon Abri meant 'My Refuge' she had found, when looking up the word in her French dictionary. Some refuge! she thought, her lips twisting. But she could make it attractive if she cleared everything out and started again. She could afford to do it. The house in St John's Wood, where she had lived with her mother, had been sold, and her bank account was looking very healthy. She could easily cover the cost of refitting this house in a modest style. She could design everything herself, use it as a show house, and perhaps start her career as an interior decorator, something she had always dreamed of. And on the French Riviera too! Excitement ran through her like strong wine, and she began to think of colours and fabrics.

As she turned to go out of the room Josie's eye caught something red sticking out from under the bed. Cautiously, so as not to disturb the dust, she pulled it out and found it was a child's toy, a felt donkey with one leg missing and a red plastic saddle. Like everything else, it was covered with dust. Josie stood holding the pathetic object, her eyes soft, imagining the grief of the child who had left it behind and had wept for its loss.

She carried it downstairs and out on to the terrace, shaking and patting it to remove most of the dust. She felt that it was lucky, a good omen to tell her that all would be well in the end. She tried to make the donkey stand up on the table, but it couldn't balance on its three legs. She would make it a new leg, she thought. A piece of grey flannel and some stuffing was all she would need.

But first of all she must clear matters up with Leon.

She couldn't plan anything while her mind was confused. She held up the donkey. 'What can I do, Donk? No, you don't know. Neither do I.' She patted the donkey and laid it down again on the table. All she could do was to wait until Leon got back, and then she would find out whether he had found a cleaner. If he hadn't she would borrow a Hoover and cleaning materials and tackle the bedroom herself.

She gave it up, put on her sunglasses and studied the steeply descending garden below. That would need attending to, but not now, not today. She leaned back her head and closed her eyes. The sun got hotter and hotter, but under the vine-draped canopy it felt like lying in a warm bath. This is what a holiday is all about, Josie thought. 'No need to worry, it'll all come right, won't it Donk?' She reached for the donkey and put it on her knee before she drifted contentedly into a light sleep.

'Wake up, Sleeping Beauty.'

Josie opened her eyes to see Leon walking towards her along the terrace. Her heart gave a great thump, and then settled down to beat rather fast. It was just surprise at seeing him unexpectedly, she assured herself.

He sank down into the chair next to her, lowering the two shopping bags he was carrying on to the floor.

Josie sat up, blinking herself fully awake. 'Oh, it's you. I—I didn't hear the car.' She was gabbling, and she tried to pull herself together. She felt confused, as if she had had a shock. 'How did you get on?'

'First things first.' He leaned down and took a large

bottle of lemonade from one of the bags. 'Will you be very sweet and get some glasses from the kitchen.'

She got up and went into his kitchen. When she got back with the glasses and some ice-cubes from the fridge, Leon was holding the donkey. 'Where did you find this little fellow?' he asked.

She took the toy from him. 'Under one of the beds. Isn't he sweet? I'm going to make a new leg for him.'

'Clever girl.' Leon poured lemonade into the two glasses, added ice and they drank in silence.

He stood up, lifting the carrier bags with one hand. 'Come along inside and you can see what I've bought for lunch. By the way, I've booked a plumber and cleaner. They should be here any minute.'

'Oh, you found help? You didn't say.'

The dark brows rose. 'Didn't I? But I told you I would arrange it.'

She nodded. 'I forgot that you always get what you want.' She put a cutting edge to the words.

They were in the kitchen now, and he dropped the bags and gripped her arm. 'Friends—have you forgotten already?'

She couldn't help laughing at the pained expression on his face. 'Sorry,' she said. 'I should have said that you must have a magic wand to make people do your bidding.'

'That's more like it,' he said. 'Although I don't see myself as the Fairy King. Don't worry, you'll soon get accustomed to seeing me as a friend, not an enemy.'

She laughed again. 'That was how I thought of you

at first, when you...you...' She broke off, the blood running into her cheeks.

'When I kissed you?' Leon put in softly. He looked down at her pink cheeks and added, 'That was the result of a mistake on my part.' He was silent for a few moments, then he added teasingly, 'But friends may kiss too, you know.'

And before she could take in the full implication of the words he drew her towards him and kissed her on the lips. 'Like this,' he murmured against her mouth.

When he lifted his head she couldn't think of a word to say. All her confused mind was telling her was that she wanted to throw her arms round his neck and kiss him back.

She was saved from doing anything so crazy when the loud chugging and spluttering of a powerful motorbike crunching along the gravel sounded from outside. 'That'll be my plumber friend,' Leon said. 'I'll go and put him in the picture.' He strode towards the front door, adding over his shoulder 'You'd better come along too.'

She stared after him. He could change so quickly from smiling tenderly at her to issuing brusque orders.

She sighed. She supposed the brusqueness was safer, and she would have to encounter plenty of it in the next week. Friendship, she told herself. Hold on to that, Josie, for it's all you will get from Leon. She had to remember that for a week. And, whatever happened then, whoever Mon Abri belonged to, they would part and she wouldn't ever see him again.

A dull ache seemed to have settled in her chest.

CHAPTER FOUR

THE motorcycle was still panting and snarling when Josie joined Leon. When the noise stopped, and the massive machine came to a shuddering halt beside Leon's car, a woman in a flowered dress slid off the pillion seat, pulling off her helmet. She was very thin and tall. The rider divested himself of his crash helmet, took a beret from the pocket of his blue overalls and, getting up to pull the heavy machine on to its stand, looked up at Leon. He was as small as the woman was tall—a little plump man, who looked about half the size of his companion. Standing side by side they made a very odd pair.

'Bonjour, m'sieur, m'selle.' He swivelled his gaze to Josie and back again. *'Moi, je suis Gaston.'* Then, indicating the lanky woman beside him, he added, *'Et voici ma petite soeur, Hortense.'*

My little sister! Josie had to choke back a giggle, and, glancing up at Leon, she saw that he, too, was appreciating the joke. The way his mouth curved up at the corners and the amusement in the look that passed between them did more to cement their new friendship than any words or any playful kiss could.

Gaston burst into a torrent of rapid French, of which Josie didn't understand more than a word here and there. School A-level French had never been like this. She smiled up at the tall Hortense and tried a few welcoming words. She was quite sure from that lady's voluble reply that there couldn't be any communication between them. She gave Leon a helpless glance.

He turned from conversing with Gaston in what sounded like perfect French. 'Hortense doesn't speak any English, Gaston tells me. Can you cope with her?'

'No,' Josie gasped, in a voice that brought a grin to Leon's face.

'Like me to take over?'

'Oh, yes, please.' How could she ever have imagined she could manage without him?

'OK, I'll get them both going. Hortense can clean up the main bedroom and the shower-room for you, and Gaston will take a look at the plumbing. He glanced at his watch. 'They'll only do a couple of hours today. They'll be off home for their siesta. But they'll come and finish tomorrow.' He turned back to Gaston with more rapid and—to Josie—unintelligible directions.

Josie made her way back into the next-door kitchen. The little woman back in her proper place, she thought with a rueful smile. Oh, well, at least Leon couldn't handle a bread knife.

As she began to unload the shopping bags on to the worktop Leon passed outside the kitchen window, followed by Hortense. A few minutes later they both marched back, Hortense leading the way, carrying a large scrubbing brush and a bar of soap, Leon behind her swinging a red plastic bucket full of steaming hot water. As he passed the window he caught Josie's eye and gave her a broad wink. This week, she thought, was promising to be more fun than she had expected.

By the time Leon came back she had put everything away and cleared up the kitchen. He leaned against the doorpost, eyeing her with amusement. 'The *patois* was too much for you?'

She grimaced. 'I thought I could cope with the language, but I couldn't understand a word of it.' She gave him an enquiring look.

'I'm not surprised,' he told her. 'They speak a *patois* down here. I'm familiar with it myself. My mother is French and she came from this district. She used to chatter away to me in *patois*, and a child picks up languages very quickly.' He walked across the kitchen and stood looking out of the window, hands in pockets. 'Also, I spent many holidays in Menton with my grandmother, when she was alive, bless her.' He sighed. 'She died eight years ago. That seems a long time ago, but somehow I remember those holidays as if they'd just been yesterday. I've always loved this place, and now I've come back here I find I still do. That's why—' He broke off, resting his hands on the worktop, staring ahead unseeingly.

Josie glanced at him and thought that she had never seen him look sad before. Angry, frustrated, irritable, patronising, teasing—yes, but not sad. It changed him completely, softened his rather hard face, pulled his mouth into a tender, relaxed line. For a moment Josie almost weakened in her resolve to keep Mon Abri for herself. She, too, had had a beloved grandmother, and she thought she knew how he felt. She had a ridiculous urge to tell him that she had changed her mind, just to see his smile break out.

She pulled herself together. That wouldn't do at all. 'You must tell me all about your holidays some time,' she said. 'Meanwhile, what's the news from the cleaning department?'

He roused himself. 'Oh, Hortense takes it very seriously. Already she has the mattress and bedclothes out in the sun, and the rest of the room is going to be thoroughly scrubbed with soap and water. I'm sorry if that isn't the right treatment for the furniture, but as you said you intended to clear everything out if you keep the house I thought it wouldn't matter, and at least it will be clean. Hortense plans to scrub the shower-room next, and is coming back tomorrow to finish upstairs and clean up the sitting-room. 'Gaston doesn't think there is much wrong with the pipe— merely a broken joint. He's putting that right.' He shook his head over the general plumbing of Mon Abri. 'We agreed that the partition of the original villa was a DIY job. It shouldn't be difficult to take it all down—if necessary.' He met her eyes innocently.

Pointedly ignoring the remark, she took down the bag of ground coffee she had just put away in one of the cupboards. 'Would you like some coffee?'

He grinned at her. 'That's a question you never need ask a Frenchman. Shall we have it outside?' He wandered out to the terrace.

She watched him go. She would make coffee as a Frenchman would like it, she thought. Not from a jar of instant such as she had made for breakfast. Fortunately the filter coffee machine was similar to the one she had used in the flat, and she spooned what she thought was enough into the filter, added water and switched on. When the jug was full she filled two small cups with coffee. She looked down at them dubiously. It really did look very strong. She took a sip from one of the cups. Ugh! She couldn't drink that. Pouring half of it into the sink, she filled the cup up with milk and left it in the kitchen. The other cup she carried out to the terrace and set down at Leon's side. 'Try that,' she said, 'and tell me if it's OK.'

He sipped the coffee. 'Excellent,' he said. 'Just how I like it.' He glanced across the table. 'Where's yours?'

She felt her cheeks go pink, as if she'd been found guilty of some crime. 'Well—I—' she stammered.

She saw the crinkles of amusement beside Leon's eyes. 'How much did you pour down the sink?' he enquired blandly.

Josie sighed gustily. 'About half of it,' she admitted. 'How did you know?'

'Just a guess,' he said. 'I reckon I can tell if a girl really enjoys black coffee or if she's trying to appear sophisticated. I was sure you weren't a black coffee girl.'

Josie glared at him. 'I don't care to be psychoanalysed,' she said shortly. 'I shall take coffee to the work brigade.' She went back into the kitchen and poured two more cups. These she carried through the front door and along the paved path to the next house.

Gaston was leaning against a ladder, a Gauloise hanging from the side of his mouth. From above came the sound of vigorous scrubbing. That figures, thought

Josie darkly. She held out one of the cups. *'Pour votre soeur,'* she said, glancing upwards. He took the cup and put it down on the ladder, while he thanked Josie and began to drink his own. Yes, she thought as she walked back the way she had come. Men were selfish; they took what they wanted. That was what Leon intended to do, but this time he was going to be disappointed.

Back in the kitchen, she drank the cup of tepid coffee. Then she went through the sitting-room and out on to the terrace.

Leon had pushed aside his cup and was making drawings on a pad of paper. She went up behind him silently and looked over his shoulder to see if he had started to make plans for the villa's refurbishment. How long and slender his fingers were, yet there was controlled strength in the way they grasped the pencil. She stared down, not noticing the marks he made so surely across the page, seeing only the moving hand and the way the dark hair grew in a fuzz along his forearms. When, suddenly, he turned and looked up at her their faces were only inches apart, and their eyes met and held for what seemed a long, long moment.

Josie felt her pulse quicken, and she wondered what she was doing, exchanging soulful looks like this with a man who was still little more than a stranger. He was the first to look away, and she slid into a chair, her heart thudding.

'I was admiring your skill,' she said, hoping he wouldn't notice the unsteadiness of her voice.

He pushed the pad away. 'Plenty of time for that

later. And I must tell you that I had no thought of psychoanalysing you. I was paying you a compliment.'

She was growing accustomed to his habit of returning to a conversation as if it hadn't been broken.

'Oh, yes?' she murmured, her throat still tight.

'Yes. I should have added that I wasn't trying to make you look silly, but admiring your honest admission.' He grinned. 'Now, let's be serious. Would you like to come down to the town after lunch? I could show you some of the sights. Or do you know Menton already?'

'No,' Josie said. 'I've never been here before, and I'd love to take a closer look at the famous Mediterranean. And I must hire a little car; I can't be dependent on you.'

He was looking at her rather oddly. She couldn't tell whether he was annoyed, or pleased he was to be relieved of her company. 'Shouldn't you leave that until the end of the week, when you know better what you will be doing?'

She lifted her chin and gave him a straight look. 'I know exactly what I shall be doing,' she said in a dignified tone. 'And why are you always referring to it? Are you trying to brainwash me and convince me that I'm not the owner of Mon Abri?'

He frowned. 'Do I do that? Perhaps I'm trying to convince myself that it will be mine.'

Something in his voice made her look curiously at him. 'Does it mean all that much to you?' He was staring in silence down the steep slope of neglected garden, and again there was the unfamiliar sad expression in his eyes. There was something more than nostalgia here, Josie realised.

At last he said slowly and heavily, 'Yes, it does.'

It would have been so easy to say, Why? And she might have learnt something about his family. But it would have been impertinent, and anyway he wouldn't have answered.

He stood up. 'Come along, let's go and interview Gaston.' He took her arm and they walked together along the terrace.

In Mon Abri, Leon acted as interpreter and Josie was told that Gaston had done all he could do to the plumbing and that the water was now turned on. He showed Leon how the hot water supply was managed in the kitchen, and then they went upstairs to learn how the shower worked. Hortense was just finishing scrubbing the bedroom, and when Josie had learned all about the heater in the shower-room she went along to see the result.

Every inch of the room had been scrubbed, and it smelled clean and fresh. Josie wanted to express her satisfaction and tried, *'C'est magnifique. Merci bien.'* accompanied by a bright smile. Hortense seemed to be pleased, and nodded and smiled back. Then she went off to scrub the shower-room.

Josie collected the two coffee cups and went back to the next-door kitchen, leaving Leon talking to Gaston. She looked at her watch. She might as well prepare lunch now, and then they could have it when they wanted to. She sliced baguettes in half and put the two halves together with butter and prawns, tiny onions and sprigs of lettuce, the whole sprinkled with a vinaigrette dressing. She repeated the process twice more, and then divided each portion into two and arranged the lot on an oval dish. These, with little cakes and fruit, should be enough for lunch. She'd found a tray, and was transferring the food on to it, when Leon came back.

He surveyed the tray with interest. 'The lady may not speak the *patois* but she's a wizard in the kitchen,' he remarked. 'I think I'm beginning to feel hungry.' He picked up a bottle of wine and started to open it. 'Wine or lemonade?'

'Oh, lemonade, please.' Josie took ice cubes from the freezer compartment, slid them into a glass basin and carried the tray out to join Leon, wondering, not for the first time, how it was that the kitchen in this side of the house was so well appointed, with all mod cons, while poor Mon Abri seemed more or less destitute of everything except three mugs. She began to make a list in her mind of what she would need immediately.

When she joined Leon she asked him whether he could throw light on the mystery, but he shook his head in an uninterested way, and when she began to talk about shopping for essential items he said lazily, pouring wine into his glass, 'Oh, you don't want to bother about fitting up the next-door kitchen. We're sharing mine until the end of the week. You'll have your own bedroom and shower-room. What more do you want?'

She didn't want to start arguing with him. And she didn't suppose that men were interested in kitchen things.

They ate lunch slowly. It was too hot to talk and Josie vowed that the subject of the two houses should not be referred to. She bit thoughtfully into a delicious little cake and let her mind wander. What a strange, unsatisfactory situation they were in! Surely a man and a girl alone together would have so many questions to ask, so much that each wanted to know about the other. But she and Leon were strangers, thrown together by circumstance, not by their own wishes. He knew practically nothing about her and she knew nothing at all about him, except that he had loved a grandmother who had lived in Menton.

Her musings were interrupted by the snarls of a motorbike being violently kick-started.

Leon sat up. 'They're off,' he said as the motor started and chugged up the short drive on the other side of the house. 'Now we're free to please ourselves. I suggest we both partake of a siesta before starting off. It will be grilling down in the town. The room you had last night faces the other way and should be more comfortable than it is out here. You go along and have a rest until it's time to start off— about three.'

He was issuing orders again, but she had to admit that they made sense.

Upstairs, in the room she had slept in for half of last night, it was much cooler than on the terrace. She stripped off and pulled on the light gown she had dried in the sun. In the bathroom she revelled in a cool shower and washed the dust out of her hair. It would dry by itself before it was time to leave. Towelling it briskly, she went back to the bedroom.

Here she searched in her bag for something to wear. She felt a faint thrill of excitement at the prospect of visiting Menton with Leon at her side. It was a long time since she had been out with a man and it was only natural, she told herself, that she should want to look her best. Unfortunately she was woefully short of clothes.

Sorting through her bag, she threw out the items to be washed, and was left with a choice between a red sundress with white stripes and a silk sheath in dark cream, which the salesgirl had assured her went wonderfully with her russet hair. She laid the cream dress on a chair, together with clean underclothes and matching sandals, made a neat pile of the soiled clothes and then, throwing off her gown, lay sprawled out luxuriously on the soft bed. She wasn't going to have a bed like this to sleep on tonight, so she might as well make the most of it. She yawned, stretched, and in less than five minutes was fast asleep.

She was wakened by a faint noise which she couldn't place. She sat up, listening, but the noise was not repeated and there was no other sound. What had it been? It had sounded like the click of a lock, as if the door had been quietly closed. She felt her cheeks get hot. Had Leon looked in to see if she was ready? With horror she saw from her watch that it was just after three o'clock. She must have slept like the dead for almost an hour. Grabbing her gown, and pulling the sash tightly round her, she crossed the room to the door. When she opened it and peered round cautiously she saw and heard nothing. The door of Leon's room was half open and all was silent inside. She had been dreaming. She wished she could be sure, but decided firmly that she must forget all about it and hurry to get dressed. Leon was probably waiting for her downstairs.

He was standing on the terrace and he turned as she joined him. 'Ah, there you are!' He consulted his watch. 'Only ten minutes late—not bad.' He ran his eyes over her from head to toe. 'And looking very charming, too.'

'Thank you,' she said. She couldn't meet his eyes. She tried to thrust away the embarrassing picture that was still in her mind of Leon standing beside the bed looking down at her naked body, just as he had stood on that other humiliating occasion. She had to know, but she couldn't think how to ask him without seeming to accuse him of something.

He regarded her quizzically. 'Did I wake you up? I came to your door to see if you were ready and when you didn't answer I opened the door a crack and peeped in. You seemed to be fast asleep so I left you to it. I thought you needed sleep after last night's goings on.' He was still watching her face. He grinned. 'Only a little peep, honest!'

She met his eyes then, and her lips quivered into a rueful little smile. She said haltingly, 'It—it's just that I heard the door close and I couldn't help remembering...'

He gripped her arm and gave it a shake. 'Forget it,' he said. 'We must leave all that behind us. We're friends now, Josie, and we're going down to Menton to look at the Mediterranean. Right?'

As he went back to lock the French window she

looked after him. He had changed into black fitted trousers and a snowy white shirt. His crisp dark hair was brushed tidily, and when he turned and smiled at her he looked so fabulous that she caught her breath. But she had to keep up the charade of being just friends. 'You look very smart yourself,' she said mischievously.

He bowed. 'In fact we make a handsome couple. We'll take the natives by storm in Menton. Shall we get going, then? I've locked up at the front.'

Five minutes later they were in Leon's long black car, swooping down the steep hill into the town. At the bottom, Leon pointed out a large low building. 'That's the local supermarket,' he said. 'We'll call there on the way back if we need any more provisions. I'm going to drive on and park somewhere in the old town, and then we can be tourists and stroll along the promenade. OK?'

'OK!' agreed Josie, living for the moment and not thinking ahead. She was going to enjoy herself.

But wouldn't it be wonderful, she thought rather wistfully, if Leon was a man she had met recently and this was their first date, with the day ahead full of promise? She sighed.

Leon looked down at her quickly. 'Something wrong?' he queried.

She smiled back brilliantly. 'No, everything's lovely. I'm just drinking in the air.' It was as good an excuse as any.

Leon didn't reply, but he put a hand briefly on her knee. 'I think I understand how you feel,' he said quietly.

Josie felt the blood surging into her face and turned her head to stare through the car window. He couldn't guess how she felt about him. He *couldn't*. Why, she didn't even know herself. No, he must have guessed that there was somebody else—some other man—she was missing. She remembered that he had seen her put the silver-framed snapshot of her mother into her bag when she was flooded out, and afterwards had made a pointed remark about it. Well, if he imagined she was yearning for some unknown man, that would suit her, and help her to get through the week of 'friendship'.

It would be too embarrassing if he guessed that she was in the greatest danger of falling in love with him.

CHAPTER FIVE

WHEN Leon had found a parking place, Josie slid out of the car and looked about her, fascinated. From where she was standing the old town rose up and up, a huddle of white and orange buildings. Highest of all, a spire pointed dramatically into the sky.

'That's the church up there, isn't it? Could we walk up and look at it?' she suggested.

Leon took her arm and steered her away. 'Some other time. You've no idea what a climb it would be in this heat. We'd be laid out panting before we got up there.' Instead he led her on, the way they had come, past an open space framed by tall palm trees where a group of old men were playing their favourite game—boules—and shouting noisily with encouragement or disgust. Josie couldn't tell which. They looked so typically French, in their berets with their Gauloises drooping from the corners of their mouths, that she chuckled.

She was still smiling when they reached the place where a road, busy with cars, ran along parallel to the sea front. There was a promenade on the seaward side, and Josie looked with delight at the wide, dark blue sweep of the bay dotted with bobbing white and red sails. A chatter of voices and laughter came from the strollers along the promenade. She supposed you would call it crowded unless you were used to the crowds in London. Some people sat at small tables, shaded by huge raffia umbrellas. The tables were arranged in groups along the promenade, close to the railings, giving the appearance of an outdoor café. Josie looked again and saw that it *was* a café. But where did the food and drink come from?

As she wondered she saw a young waiter, carrying a loaded tray, run across the road, dodging the cars, to serve his customers on the promenade, then dart back again. The cafés themselves were on the opposite side of the road.

Josie stopped, holding her breath, when she saw the young men apparently risking life and limb, but Leon laughed at her and said it was a job like any other job and they were professionals. 'You're too softhearted,' he teased.

As they strolled along together Josie was suddenly very conscious that Leon was still holding her arm. The touch of his hand against her bare skin disturbed her and made her pull away a little to rest a hand against the railing and look around at the whole vista.

'Oh, how lovely it is,' she breathed, gazing at a boulevard joining the road on the right. The wide central space was almost a park in itself, shimmering in the sunlight with flowers of all colours. Tall palm trees grew on either side, and down the centre there were small trees at intervals which must be lemon trees, for Josie saw tiny green lemons on the branches.

'The casino is just over there,' Leon told her, his eyes following her gaze. 'There's a station at the top of the hill. The original idea was that travellers who had just arrived by rail would be charmed by the beauty of the place as they came down the hill, probably in horse-drawn carriages.'

'Well, *I'm* certainly charmed by it, even without a horse-drawn carriage,' Josie said, turning again towards the sweep of blue water. 'It's a heavenly place.'

A light breeze ruffled her russet curls and whipped up the colour in her cheeks. Her hazel eyes sparkled with delight.

Leon was standing with his back to the rails, leaning both elbows on them and watching Josie's face with an odd little smile playing round his mouth. When she turned to share her pleasure with him the look in his eyes made her feel confused. She tried to think of something to say but could think of nothing.

She was saved from saying anything when a smartly dressed middle-aged woman who was hurrying past stopped suddenly with a little gasp of surprise. 'Leon!' she cried. 'Leon Kent! It *is* you, isn't it?' She took a step towards him, holding out both her hands. 'This is wonderful. We've so often talked of you and wondered how you were getting on. I suppose you're a fully-fledged architect now.'

'Mrs. Martin—my good angel!' Leon took her hands and kissed her on both cheeks. 'What a happy coincidence. We were going to look you up and find out if you were still in Menton.' He turned to Josie 'This is Josie Dunn, Charles Dunn's daughter. She is an interior designer and we are staying at the villa, making some plans for doing the place up.'

Mrs Martin held out her hand to Josie with a warm smile. 'We knew your father quite well—we rented the villa from him for many years. Our lease was up last year and we decided to move down into the town.' She added to Leon, 'Jonathan and family had already moved out, a year before us. They have two children now, and Mon Abri was too small for them when the new baby came along.' She looked towards Josie. 'Your father and his wife spent a long holiday at the villa after we left, last summer, but I don't think there has been anyone living at either place since then.'

If Mon Abri had been empty for nearly two years that would explain its neglected condition, Josie thought, whereas Charles would have spared nothing to keep the main house well-equipped, especially if the holiday was a final attempt to hold a shaky marriage together. Josie couldn't help feeling glad that it had failed.

'And how is Caroline? Quite grown-up now, I suppose,' Leon was enquiring.

'Oh, goodness, yes. She's nearly twenty-one. She has a job in Monte Carlo—on the reception at one of the hotels.' A frown creased Mrs Martin's forehead and her soft mouth firmed. 'I'm not keen on her being there, I wish she'd taken a job near home, but she seems to love it. She shares a flat with two of the other girls and drives her own little car, which means that she can get home easily. I'll tell her I've met you; she'd love to come up to the villa to see you, although you won't recognise her as the plump little girl you knew all those years ago.' She glanced at her watch. 'Heavens, I must fly. I'm late for a dental appointment as it is. You must both come and have a meal with us, then we can exchange all our news. Andrew is retired now, and crazy about sailing. We're off to Paris for a couple of days, but we'll be in touch when we get back. You'll still be at the villa?'

'For the next week at least,' Leon said, without looking at Josie. 'Yes, we'd love to come.'

Mrs Martin handed Leon a card from the clutch bag she was holding, and after a hasty *au revoir* ran lightly across the road between the cars. Having reached the opposite side, she turned and waved before disappearing up the boulevard.

Josie watched her go and said, 'She's nice, isn't she, your Mrs Martin? She doesn't look old enough to have a grown-up family.'

Leon said, 'Probably not. But even when I was here, years ago, she was old enough to keep them both well in order. Jonathan was just about to get married and she was installing them in Mon Abri. Fortunately his wife was very young and quite docile and so no sparks flew. I imagine quite a few sparks are flying now, between Mama and young Caroline, who showed signs of having a mind of her own. She also showed signs of growing into a beauty when she lost her puppy fat. It will be amusing to see how she has grown up. You won't mind dining with them?'

'Of course not,' Josie said. 'It's always fun to meet people you've heard about.'

Leon nodded, and dismissed the subject. There was a vacant table just ahead of them and he suggested that they should have a cool drink and eat some of the little cakes which Josie had shown a liking for at lunch. 'If you can manage to harden that heart of yours when a waiter risks all in your service,' he added with a smile.

The rest of the afternoon passed too quickly for Josie, who enjoyed it all as she had resolved to do. They wandered round the new part of the town and Leon pointed out the tall house where his grandmother had lived. 'She was a darling,' he said, his eyes soft. 'My sister and I had some wonderful holidays here.'

Josie insisted on being shown the shops where she could stock up with new clothes. One shop in particular caught her fancy—a small boutique in a side-road. Josie lingered before the window, admiring the one dress there—a chic little number in primrose-yellow silk jersey. She looked up at Leon, who was watching her with an amused smile. 'Well, why don't you go in and buy it?' he said.

She gasped. 'You're a thought-reader.'

'No, but you have a very expressive face.'

'Oh dear, I'll have to watch it,' Josie chuckled. 'But as it happens you're right this time. Do you mind waiting?'

'If I can see you in that dress I'll wait with considerable enjoyment,' he said with his wicked grin. 'Come along, let's go in.' He opened the door for her and followed her inside. Josie looked round appreciatively at the colour scheme of white with celery-green, pale enough to make an interesting background for any other colour without intruding.

Madame came forward, an imposing woman in black, her dark hair parted severely in the middle and forming an intricate arrangement on top of her head.

'*Bonjour, m'sieur, mademoiselle,*' she greeted them, after a quick glance at Josie's left hand. Josie felt a small pang. If only she *was* Leon's wife and he was buying a dress for her.

When Josie came back from the fitting-cubicle behind the shop Madame made little coos of pleasure. '*M'selle est ravissante, n'est ce pas, m'sieur?*' Josie caught sight of herself in the long mirror. The 'dress' was actually a two-piece affair. The skirt moulded her neat hips and fluted out around her legs. The top had narrow shoulder-straps and was very low-cut. And there was a gauzy wide scarf which was almost exactly the colour of her hair.

Josie turned to Leon, laughing. 'I love the outfit, even without the compliment. Yes, *madame*,' she added in her careful French, 'I should like to buy it.' And Leon added something in French so rapid that she couldn't follow.

As she went back to the cubicle to change she saw Leon taking out his chequebook. That completed the illusion, Josie grinned to herself.

Ten minutes later they emerged from the boutique, Josie carrying an elaborate dress-box. She said, 'Thank you for standing by. I'll repay you with traveller's cheques, if that's OK with you. And what was the long speech you made to Madame?'

He said casually, 'Oh, I agreed that you were ravishing. And I said you looked like a primrose with the dew on it in a green meadow.'

She looked up at him mischievously from under long lashes. 'I thought you were an architect—someone who deals in slide-rules and set-squares—not a poet who has pretty visions.'

He linked his arm with hers as they walked along. 'Oh, I do have my visions occasionally. And I don't think modern poetry is like that now.'

They argued about modern poetry until they were finally back to where they had left the car. Leon drove back past the crowded marina to the supermarket, where Josie bought a chicken dish which could be reheated in the oven and vegetables for supper, while Leon prowled round the wine department and joined her carrying a large bag filled with bottles. 'We'll get home now, shall we, and open one of these?' He indicated the bag.

Home! If only it were! She had allowed a dream to take over the whole afternoon. Leon drove up the twisty hill and through the gate at the top of the short drive. As he reached the car park Josie saw that there was a small red car there already. Leon switched off the engine and frowned at the red car. 'Who the hell's this? I'm not expecting guests—are you?'

Josie shook her head, and he got out of the car and took the bags from the back, muttering under his breath, 'Oh, well, I suppose we'd better go and find out.'

Josie took her dress-box from the back seat and followed him round the side of the house and on to the terrace. A fair girl who had been sitting at the table got up and came forward, holding out both hands. 'Leon! Have you forgotten me?'

'Caroline!' Leon dropped both bags and took the girl's hands, drawing her towards him. His back was towards Josie, and she didn't know whether he kissed the girl, but the pleasure in his voice sent a twinge of jealousy through her.

Leon held the girl at arm's length. 'My, how you've grown!' It was just the way he teased *her*, Josie thought dully, and immediately became aware of all the other girls he must have teased in just the same way.

The girl gave a gurgle of laughter. 'Haven't I just? No longer your little Podge.' They laughed together delightedly.

Josie looked at the house for somewhere to hide herself, but all the doors and windows were, she knew, locked. So she stood still, feeling very much in the way, until Leon turned and held out a hand to her. 'This is Caroline Martin, Josie,' he said. 'We met her mother this afternoon. Caroline, meet Josie Dunn, who is helping me with my work on the house.'

The two girls regarded each other. Josie put her dress-box down and smiled and said 'Hello.' The other girl said, 'Hi,' without much interest, and turned back to Leon.

'I drove over to see Ma and Pa before they left for Paris. Ma told me about meeting you and I just had to come up here before I drove back to Monte Carlo. Did Ma tell you I'm a receptionist now? Hence the uniform.' She was wearing a plum-coloured suit with a white blouse. The skirt was straight, and extremely short, and when she struck a pose to show herself off to Leon she disclosed what seemed like yards of tanned legs.

She turned to Josie. 'Ma told me that Leon had

someone helping him. You design things, don't you? You must be very clever.' She pulled a rueful face as she looked back to Leon. 'All I can do is smile at visitors and check bookings and hand out keys. But I never was clever, was I, darling?'

With her looks she didn't have to be clever, Josie thought, watching her as she shook back her golden mane of hair and grinned audaciously up at Leon. She was very lovely, Josie had to admit, with her cloud of gold hair, her huge blue eyes and her perfect, faintly tanned skin. And men weren't supposed to like clever girls anyway, were they?

Leon parked the shopping bags and put an arm around each girl. 'Let's all go and sit down. I'll open a bottle to celebrate our meeting after all this time, Podge.'

Caroline gave a disgusted snort as Leon said to Josie, 'Caroline used to be a fat girl once, didn't you, sweetheart?' He gave the girl's slim waist a squeeze. 'I always told your mother that you'd end up a beauty—and so you have.'

Caroline rubbed her cheek against him. 'I simply love compliments. Does that mean you've waited all this time for me, darling Leon, as you promised?'

Leon groaned, 'Ah, promises, promises.'

As they all sat down he turned and explained to Josie, 'When this lovely girl was twelve—or was it thirteen?—she made me promise to wait to marry her until she grew up.'

'And you did wait,' Caroline purred. 'I'm sure you did, didn't you? The truth, now.' She put a hand on Leon's arm.

This was just airy nonsense, Josie thought. But when Leon disengaged his arm from Caroline's grasp and stretched out to put a hand over her own hand, saying, 'You couldn't expect me to when there are so many pretty girls around—like this one,' she felt that the game had gone far enough. Leon was making her look foolish, and she didn't like it. She tried to pull her hand away, but he was still holding it firmly.

Caroline thinned her lips and gave Josie a look that was verging on contempt. 'So that's the way it is, is it?'

Leon ignored that remark, saying they would drink a toast to the reunion of old friends. He unlocked the French window and carried the two bags into the kitchen, returning with a bottle of white wine, three glasses and a corkscrew. Josie noticed the way Caroline's eyes followed him. Did she really intend to try to keep him to his promise? She felt another quick stab of jealousy.

He consulted the label on the bottle before pulling the cork, pouring a small amount of wine into a glass and tasting it. 'Not bad. Not quite what I wanted, but not bad at all.'

'Don't show off, darling,' Caroline teased, and he pulled a face at her and filled all three glasses.

Caroline drank her wine in three gulps, looking at her watch. 'I must go now—this minute,' she said. 'This is just a flying visit. We have this shift arrangement on Reception, and I'm supposed to be on at seven. But I just had to come up and take a look at you first. You simply must come to Monte Carlo. I have part of Friday evening free and we can have fun.' She glanced at Josie and added, 'You, too, if you like. I'll bring another man.' She waved a casual hand and hurried along the terrace towards the car park. Leon got up and followed her.

Josie stayed where she was, seething gently with rage. How dared Leon behave as he had done? Letting the girl think that they were living here together as—as partners. Friendship didn't extend to this sort of behaviour, and he must make the situation clear to Caroline when he saw her. She herself had no intention of going with him to Monte Carlo. She felt a pang of regret. She would have loved to see the famous Casino if things had been different. *Why* had he behaved so absurdly? She meant to find out.

Leon seemed to be away a long time, in spite of the fact that Caroline was supposed to be in a hurry, but at last she heard the sound of the little car driving off, and a few moments later he returned and flopped into the chair beside her. He was smiling broadly. 'A lovely little bit of nonsense, don't you think?'

She met his smiling eyes coldly. 'I was too cross to take very much notice.'

He pulled a wry face. 'Oh, dear, what have I done now?'

'It's not a joke,' she said. 'You let that girl think that we—that you and I are living here together.'

'Well, we are, aren't we?' he said mildly.

She glared at him, hazel eyes sparking green with fury. 'Of course we're not. Not in the way she chose to take it.'

'Oh, Josie, dear, calm down. Where's your sense of humour? You wouldn't like Caroline to believe that

I really had waited for her, would you? I needed an alibi.'

Her anger was coming to the boil. 'I don't give a—give a damn what you needed. You put me in a false position and I hate it.' Tears of humiliation stung behind her eyes. 'Why did you have to bring me in? Merely *friends*,' she reminded him. 'And please make that clear to Caroline when you see her.'

He put a hand over his heart. 'I promise. I'll make sure she hasn't got the wrong impression. You can witness it yourself on Friday night, when we go to Monte Carlo.'

'I won't be coming,' she said shortly. She stood up. 'Now, if you'll please give me the keys, I'll go in and see what has to be done in my bedroom before I cook supper.'

She picked up the dress-box and they walked together in silence through the house to the front door. When Leon had unlocked it he took a key from his pocket and handed it to Josie. 'It's all yours,' he said.

'Thank you,' she said frostily, and marched along the path to her own house.

A depressing smell of damp greeted her, and she made a mental note to get Gaston to put the divan out into the sun. The bedroom looked much the same as when she had last seen it. Hortense had put the mattress out on the balcony outside the window to air. Josie went out to pull it in, but it was large and thick and heavy and all she could do was to try to drag it back into the bedroom. Even this took all her strength, and she had got it only halfway into the room, and was breathing rather hard, when the door opened behind her and Leon came in, carrying the bedclothes which had been put out on the terrace to air. 'What are you trying to do, you idiotic girl? Here, let me.'

He pushed her away, grabbed the mattress with both hands and with a huge tug managed to pull it into the room.

'Stop!' yelled Josie. 'Now look what you've done.' She held his wrist to show where the blood had begun to soak through the bandage. 'I'll have to attend to that straight away,' she said. 'Come along.'

'Damn!' exploded Leon, and gave the mattress a hefty kick. It toppled over and fell flat on the floor, raising a cloud of dust. He shrugged, and followed Josie down the stairs.

In the shower-room of the next house Josie made sure Leon was sitting down before she removed the bandages. The wound was certainly bleeding, but it looked clean and she was able to apply a fresh dressing and bind up the hand again. 'That's it,' she said at last. It was the first time either of them had spoken since they left her bedroom. Glancing at him, she saw that he hadn't changed colour.

'Thank you, Josie,' he said. He reached up his right hand and pulled her hand down. Raising it to his lips, he kissed it.

When she would have pulled her hand away, he held on to it. 'I'm truly sorry,' he said. 'I must see what I can do to put things right. I'll have to think about it.'

She knew from his habit of taking up unfinished conversations that he was referring to the scene on the terrace with Caroline. There was no more to be said about that, and she made no reply. She pulled her hand away and busied herself putting the shower-room to rights while he watched her. 'Are you still cross with me?' he enquired. 'It won't make any difference to our pact of friendship, you know. And by the way, I'm afraid you'll have to accept my hospitality again tonight and sleep in my spare room. Your room in Mon Abri certainly won't be ready for you until tomorrow. You can't lift that big mattress on to the bed, and I'm sure you won't let me try, will you?'

'Of course not.' Josie wanted time to go away and think, but there was no way she could get it yet. Meanwhile she had to cook supper. But at least she could decline his offer of 'hospitality'. 'I shall sleep on the mattress on the floor,' she said. 'It wouldn't be the first time I've done that.'

'One slight problem.' He sounded rather pleased with himself. 'The mattress is full of dust. I can't risk having you down with what the medicos call a "respiratory problem".'

She was about to argue, although she didn't quite know how. He took a look at her face and continued, 'If you object to being the guest of an unmarried man I will promise to sleep on the terrace. There's a camp bed in the utility room. Or you could lock your door and believe me when I say I won't try to knock it down.'

Josie laughed almost hysterically. The whole situation was getting ridiculous.

Leon's eyes met hers, and he was laughing too. 'I thought I could trust your sense of humour,' he said. 'Now, let's go down and finish that bottle of wine.'

She shrugged. There seemed to be no way to win in any fight with this man. With a gleam in her eye she thought that matters would be reversed at the end of the week.

But did she really want them to be?

CHAPTER SIX

Josie prepared supper and set it out on the table in the kitchen. She hesitated about serving the meal on the table in the living-room. That would be more civilised, but why go to extra trouble to please Leon? That was the last thing she wanted to do as she remembered the sneering look on Caroline's face. She still went hot as she thought of it. It had been hateful of Leon to put her in such a position. It had made her feel cheap. She had registered her protest, and there was nothing more she could do about it, but she certainly was not going to Monte Carlo on Friday.

She called Leon in from the terrace, where he had been lounging, and he took his place at the table. He looked down doubtfully at his plate, piled up with chicken in mushroom sauce, new potatoes and fresh garden peas.

Josie watched him out of the corner of her eye as he struggled to eat with his fork. He managed to spear a small potato and tried to balance the peas, but the chicken defeated him and eventually he had to say, 'I'm afraid I'm back in the nursery. I'll have to ask you to cut this into manageable pieces. You bandaged my hand too tightly and I can't hold a knife.'

'Of course,' Josie said, complying. She should have felt pleasure at making him, for once, ask for help. But when he said 'Thanks,' with such a charming smile, she felt she had been mean and petty. 'I'm sorry,' she said. 'I was thinking of something else.'

He nodded. 'I wonder if I've been thinking of the same thing. We won't discuss it now. I'd hate to spoil this excellent supper. But later on I'll tell you what I believe is a good idea.'

Josie went on eating without comment. So long as his idea didn't include meeting Caroline she would consider it. To see that sneering mouth again—no, she couldn't. And the girl would tell her mother, making it into an interesting bit of scandal. So that meant that she would have to refuse Mrs Martin's invitation too.

She was still turning all this over in her mind as she cleared the dishes and put the coffee machine on. She had refused Leon's offer of brandy with her coffee, and he had taken the bottle and a glass out on to the terrace. Josie put the jug of coffee and two cups on a tray, not forgetting milk for herself. She carried the tray out to join him.

It was a beautiful warm evening. The light had almost faded, and stars were coming out to make the sky like a spangled black veil. The smell of roses came in wafts from a big, overgrown bush in the steep garden. The constant chirping of cicadas hardly seemed to disturb the peace.

Josie lay back in the cane chair and sipped her milky coffee. It would have been a perfect end to an enjoyable day if she and Leon had spent it together, free from visitors. She glanced at Leon, who had not spoken since they came out. His face was shadowy, but in the light that came through from the house she thought he looked unusually serious.

He sat up and refilled his glass. 'I must tell you my idea, Josie,' he said. 'First of all I want to say how sorry I am to have upset you with my thoughtless remark to Caroline. Thoughtless, that is, about the effect it might have on you. I'm sure that nothing I could say to her now would persuade her that you and I are "just good friends" so I'll have to tackle the problem another way. My bright idea is that you and I should get engaged to be married—for the rest of our week together. No, don't say anything yet—' as Josie began to refuse angrily '—we're stuck together here until Charles comes home and sorts out the position. And if we were engaged it would save us from any raised eyebrows from anyone, like Mrs Martin, who hasn't caught up with the modern age yet.'

'You think I'm a Victorian miss,' Josie said, lifting her chin, 'because I care what people say about me?'

He took her hand and held it lightly. 'I think you're adorable.' There was a twinkle in his eye.

Josie bit her lip. She had to get away from Leon. She couldn't think straight when he was teasing her.

He picked up the tray and carried it into the kitchen. As she followed him he said, 'No, you're not going to wash up tonight. Leave it until morning and get off to bed now. You look tired.'

Tired! Her brain was running round in circles and she felt that she would never sleep again.

'Think about my proposal and we can talk again in the morning. Goodnight, Josie.' He picked up the dress-box and put it in her hand. 'Sleep well. And please believe me when I promise that if you agree to my idea I shouldn't take advantage of the situation.'

Josie laughed unsteadily. 'No passes?'

'Definitely no passes.'

He gave her a push towards the stairs and she climbed up, murmuring, 'Goodnight,' without looking back at him.

In the bedroom, she took off her clothes and dropped them on the floor. More washing! If she didn't tackle it soon she would have nothing left to wear, she thought absently. A cool shower revived her, but did nothing to clear her brain. She had wanted time to think, but now she had plenty of time her thoughts were chaotic, and when she had finished her usual routine of hair-brushing and teeth-cleaning, and had got into her nightdress, she slipped into bed, no nearer to a solution to her problems.

She propped herself up against the pillows. She must stay awake until she had made up her mind about his suggestion that they should stage a mock engagement for what remained of their week together. At first she had burst out indignantly, but now—now she wondered. If she refused he would go off to Monte Carlo, leaving her here alone, sulking. That wasn't a pretty picture. But if they went together, and she had a diamond ring to show off to Caroline—that would be much more satisfactory. Yes, she decided firmly, she would agree, and then take things day by day. She glanced at the bedroom door. 'No passes,' he had promised, and she trusted him.

Having made a decision gave her a wonderful feeling of relaxation, and she could almost feel the tension in her head ebbing away. She put out the bedside lamp, adjusted the pillows and snuggled down into a dreamless sleep.

Josie wakened early next morning, and was downstairs in the kitchen before Leon put in an appearance. 'Good morning,' she said brightly when he came in, looking slightly tousled.

'Good morning,' he replied, holding up his bandaged hand. 'Sorry I'm late. This has rather held me up.'

'Oh, you poor darling,' smiled Josie, cutting up his bacon, 'It must be maddening for you. Never mind,' she added tenderly, 'it won't be for long.'

He gave her a suspicious look, but made no reply. She put the plate down in front of him, resting a hand on his shoulder and dropping a kiss on his untidy dark hair. She carried her own plate to the table.

He scowled. 'Look here, what's all this solicitude? It isn't like you, Josie.'

'Just practising.' She chuckled. 'You see, I haven't been engaged before, and I have to decide on the best attitude to adopt.'

'For God's sake forget about attitudes,' he growled. 'Just be yourself. I haven't been engaged before either, and I don't think I could put up with five days— or is it more?—of tender loving care.' He picked up his fork and attacked the bacon and egg. Looking up, he said, 'Does this mean that you accept my idea?'

'Oh, yes, I think it's a brilliant idea. I've only got one request.'

'Yes?' He eyed her warily.

'Just that you buy me a ring with big, flashy stones. Imitation, of course. They're quite cheap. Something to wave in front of Caroline's eyes.'

He burst out laughing. 'No problem. There's a jewellers in Menton, and I expect they sell fake as well as real stones. I'll go down and see what I can do as soon as Gaston and sister arrive.'

She nodded. 'I'd come with you, only I seem to have accumulated a pile of washing. I'll do it in the sink next door now I've got the hot water connected.'

'In the sink?' he echoed, in the bored voice of a man confronted with domestic details. 'Why not use the perfectly good washing machine in the utility room here?'

'I'd…' Josie began, intending to say that she'd prefer to live in her own house now, except for cooking the meals, but then she reminded herself that she and Leon were supposed to be living together as an engaged couple, and she said meekly, 'Thanks, I'll see if I can work it.'

At that moment Gaston's motorbike spluttered along the drive and Leon stood up, drinking down the last of his coffee. 'I'll set these two to work and then I'll be off,' he told Josie. He paused, turning back. 'I won't be long, sweetheart,' he said, grinning, and bent down to kiss her, not very briefly, on the lips. 'I rather approve of this practising idea,' he whispered. 'We'll have to do more of it.'

He walked quickly out of the room, and when she heard his car drive away, five minutes later, she was still sitting at the table, her brow creased. Her attempt to annoy him by teasing him had rebounded on herself. She might have known she couldn't win against Leon. Worse than that, she knew she was in danger— in danger of falling in love with him.

She put a finger against her lips where his own lips had lingered, and a shiver shook her. She must *not* let Leon find out. But how was she going to pretend to be in love with him when she really was in love with him? Sometimes he seemed to know what she was thinking, and if he knew he would certainly use the knowledge as a way to soften her up and persuade her to sell Mon Abri to him. She must keep reminding herself that his first object was to get her house.

She had never forgotten how he had looked when they were first discussing Mon Abri. How he had said that he expected to become the owner in a few days, and how his mouth had hardened almost brutally when he'd added, 'And I mean to have it.' He would employ any means to get what he wanted. If he believed that the house might belong to her, and his only way of owning it was to persuade her to sell it to him, what would he do? The reply was obvious. He would use all his charm to weaken her defences. Which was what he'd been doing. What a muddle the whole situation was!

She rested her elbows on the table and covered her face with her hands. Tears squeezed out of her eyes and wet her cheeks. She jumped up quickly, straightening her back and wiping her face with her handkerchief. She had seen the disastrous effects of self-pity a long time ago, when she had been caring for her mother, and she wasn't going to indulge in it now. She just had to keep reminding herself that Leon's smile, and the look that sometimes softened his eyes, were part of a deliberate ploy. She carried the dishes to the sink and washed them up. Then she walked along to Mon Abri to see how Gaston and Hortense were getting on.

She found them both in the bedroom, engaged in heaving the mattress on to the bed. After smiles and nods and *bonjours* Gaston indicated the Hoover in the corner of the room and explained in his halting English that the mattress had been cleaned and was now free from dust. He thumped it with his fist to demonstrate. Josie nodded and smiled and asked them if they would like coffee. *'Oui, oui, s'il vous plaît,'* they chorused, and she went back to the villa to put the coffee machine on, smiling to herself because they were both so nice and so anxious to help. For the first time she felt at home here.

After the coffee was delivered Josie returned to Leon's spare bedroom, which she had occupied for the last two nights. Tonight she would sleep in her own house. That should have made her satisfied, because she would be taking her first step towards independence from Leon, but instead it was like the end of a lovely holiday. She felt hollow inside as she reminded herself that at the end of a week—that would be next Wednesday—she and Leon would part, whatever the legal position, and would not meet again.

Clumsily she packed her bag, throwing in everything that belonged to her. She folded the bedclothes neatly, picked up the bag and, with a last look around the room, went out and closed the door.

Now for the washing. She found the utility room

without much trouble. It was built on to Leon's side of the house, and, with the sun pouring in through a wide window on to white-painted walls, looked cheerful and well equipped. Josie registered the fact that she must have something of the same sort built on to Mon Abri. The kitchen there was quite inadequate.

The washing machine was fortunately of the same make as the one Josie had used in St John's Wood. There was a packet of detergent on the wide counter, and within ten minutes the machine was loaded, programmed and swooshing away happily. Josie looked around, making mental notes on how her own utility room should be planned.

She was leaning down, looking into the cupboards under the counter, when suddenly she was seized from behind by two strong arms and held against a strong body. 'Hullo, sweetheart, I'm back.' Leon spoke close to her ear, held her curls away from her neck and nuzzled a kiss against it.

Taken unawares, because his steps had been drowned by the noise of the washing machine, Josie was tempted to relax and let herself be folded closer to him. But she checked herself in time and, twisting round, tried to push him away.

'I don't think you need any more practice,' she said in a slightly breathless voice. 'You're quite expert already.'

He still kept his arms around her, and, looking down into her face, said with his wicked grin, 'Maybe, but I have yet to find out whether you are.'

She pulled a face at him. 'Pooh! You won't find that out.'

'No? We shall see.'

She picked up her bag. 'I'll take this up to my own bedroom.'

'Hadn't you better wait until Gaston and Hortense have left before you take up residence? I'll help you to remove your things from my room.'

'Thanks, but I shan't need help. Everything I brought with me is either in there—' indicating the washing machine '—or in here.'

She held up her bag and turned to the door, but Leon put a hand on her arm. 'Just a minute. I've got something to give you first.' He felt in the pocket of his jeans and brought out a small box. He flicked it open and took out the ring inside. 'I couldn't find a fake one that would look convincing,' he said, 'so I'm afraid you'll have to put up with the genuine article for a few days.'

Josie looked down at the huge solitaire diamond that flashed and glittered in the sunny room and gasped. 'It's beautiful,' she said. 'But I can't possibly wear it. It would make the whole charade seem—seem...'

'As though it was real?'

'Yes—no—oh, I don't know.' She was nearly in tears. 'I wish I'd never agreed to this silly pretence. I d-don't want to come to Monte Carlo with you, wearing a ring like that, and feeling a—a fraud.'

'But you told me you wanted a flashy ring,' he said patiently.

'Yes, but only if it was a fake.'

He clicked his tongue and looked up at the ceiling.

'Women!' He replaced the ring in its box and put it back in his pocket.

'Now,' he said briskly, 'let's decide what we're going to do. I'll go along and see Gaston and Hortense first, and I'll tell Gaston to let me have their bill.'

'We must have a settling up,' Josie said. 'And I want to open a bank account here as soon as I can.'

'I'll take you along to my bank and introduce you to the manager. We can do that this afternoon.'

'Thanks,' Josie said. So again she would have to accept his help. And she had once prided herself that she was an independent girl. She would have to manage on her own when Leon had left, but she didn't want to think about that.

'And at the same time we'll go to the jewellers and you can choose a ring that you consider suitable,' Leon went on.

'Oh, I can't—' Josie began, but he brushed her words aside.

'Yes, you can,' he contradicted her cheerfully. 'And I've got another idea. We'll have lunch in Menton first and do our shopping later. We'll set off as soon as Gaston and Hortense have gone. OK?'

'OK, if I can find something to wear.'

Leon said, 'Wear that pretty cream-coloured dress you wore yesterday. It goes with your hair.' He twisted a russet curl round his finger. 'And by the way, you should have a sunhat. I could do with one too. We'll get them on our way through Menton.'

'I thought we were going to have lunch in Menton.'

'Ah, I've got a surprise for you. Wait and see.'

* * *

Things always seemed to happen exactly as Leon wanted them to, Josie reflected as she got into his car three-quarters of an hour later. He had wanted her to wear the cream dress and here she was, wearing it. The label had said 'Hand wash only' otherwise the dress would have been in the washing machine with all the rest. Josie had found it hanging in the wardrobe in Leon's spare room, with the yellow dress she had bought yesterday, and had transferred them both to her own room, where Hortense had finished her work.

As Josie had changed she'd missed the long mirror and the convenience of being able to wash in her own bedroom, but you couldn't have everything all at once, and it would be fun to install the things that were missing from Mon Abri.

In Menton they found a shop catering for visitors and Josie bought a floppy sunhat made from green cotton material with a wide stitched brim. Leon approved her choice, but told her not to pull it down too far or she would hide her pretty nose. He turned back the brim and laid a finger on the tip of her nose, laughing. He himself chose a rather odd-shaped panama, which made Josie giggle.

As they got back into the car Josie felt a sudden surge of happiness. They drove on through the town. Leon had opened the roof of the car and Josie took off her hat, laid back her head and delighted in the warmth of the sun on her face and the breeze blowing through her hair.

Presently, she realised that the car had begun to climb steeply. Up and up, sometimes making wide U-turns, and zig-zagging even higher. Josie had never encountered a drive like this, and at first felt a sense of exhilaration as the air grew cooler and she had to put on her jacket. She glanced at Leon. He was enjoying this. His eyes were narrowed and his long fingers moved easily on the wheel of the powerful car. Josie had removed the tight bandage and replaced it with a long plaster, which left his fingers free.

As they zoomed into another hairpin bend, Josie felt her ears click and her palms grow damp, and she clutched the arm of the seat. She swallowed, and said in a small voice, 'Where are you taking me? We seem to be driving up the side of a mountain.'

He chuckled. 'We're going to find an eagle's nest at the top.' Then he glanced at her. 'You're not bothered by heights, are you? What a thoughtless fool I am. I should have asked you before we started.'

Josie's stomach turned over as the car swooped into another U-bend. 'Not really,' she said, and forced a wavery laugh. 'It was such a surprise, that's all.'

'I can't turn back now,' Leon said worriedly, 'but I'll go as carefully as I can.'

It was better after that. Josie hung on to the arms of the seat and closed her eyes when they came to the bends, which he took very slowly. Up and up, higher and higher, until at last, when Josie was beginning to feel that they must have reached the top of the mountain, Leon turned off to the right, and soon afterwards took a narrow road on the left and drove on a short distance to a flat space where three cars were parked.

'We have to walk from here,' he said, getting out and opening her door for her. He took her hands to help her out of the car and stood, looking down at her. 'My poor darling, you're as white as a ghost. Let's get into the village and find a restaurant where you can be revived.'

He put an arm round her and they walked on to where there was an archway spanning the road, with little houses on either side built right into the mountain face, so that it was like walking through a tunnel. Eventually, they came out into the narrow cobbled streets of a village. Josie was beginning to feel better, and when Leon had found a quiet restaurant and set a small glass of brandy before her, she sipped it with relief.

'I expect you would rather have had wine,' Leon said. 'But I thought this would be better for you. You've got a bit more colour now. You gave me a shock when we got out of the car.'

Across the small table Josie's eyes met Leon's, and she saw something in their grey depths that sent a quiver of surprise and excitement running through her. He really did care about her. His helpfulness hadn't been simply courtesy. She blinked and looked away. 'I'm fine,' she said.

The pretty waitress came to their table with the menu card and Leon glanced at it, then handed it to Josie. 'They have a surprisingly good choice. What's your fancy?'

Josie looked at the menu, but the words danced before her eyes. She hadn't imagined that look as his eyes had rested on her. It hadn't been the look of a friend. It had been a look of love. It was impossible, she told herself, they'd only known each other a matter of days. It couldn't happen as quickly as that. But she knew that it could from the way it had happened to her. She admitted it to herself at last. That first angry kiss had started a fire inside her which had been gathering heat ever since.

She realised suddenly that Leon was waiting, and handed the menu back to him with a grimace. 'My French isn't equal to this. You'd better choose.'

While they ate their lunch Leon told her about Ste-Agnès. 'It's my favourite place,' he said. 'I wanted you to see it, but I didn't stop to wonder if you would react badly to the height; it was stupid of me.'

'It wasn't the height,' she said, quick to reassure him. 'It was all the bends and swoops.'

'Yes, I know,' he said sympathetically. 'Next time we come you'll be ready for them.'

She didn't reply. *Next time*. It seemed as if he were looking at a future together for them. She waited, holding her breath, but he went on to tell her of some of the history of Ste-Agnès and its folklore.

Josie hardly knew what she was eating, and sat listening to his stories with a smile, not hearing much of what he was saying. When they'd finished coffee Leon studied her face and said, 'How do you feel now? Equal to the famous view? I must warn you, it's quite stunning.'

She gave him a brilliant smile. 'Equal to anything.' So long as you are with me, she added to herself.

As they left the restaurant he took her hand, and they walked to where there was a small esplanade. A group of people were moving away, the women chattering in some unfamiliar language. Probably the people from the other cars, Josie thought, raising her brows towards Leon, who grinned and said, 'Tourists.'

He put an arm firmly round Josie as they leaned over the wall. Looking down, Josie gasped. The view was almost overpowering. It seemed as if the entire Côte d'Azur was spread out beneath her, the Mediterranean making a deep blue scalloped pattern against the bays and headlands. 'That must be Menton,' she said, 'although I can hardly believe it— it's so tiny. And there's the church we were looking up at yesterday.'

Her gaze travelled onto a dark green patch of wooded headland, which Leon told her was Cap Martin—'Strictly reserved for the seriously rich,' he added. Over to the right, the soaring white apartment blocks of Monte Carlo crowded densely round the bay, almost giving it the appearance of a mini-Manhattan. 'Wait until you see Monte Carlo in all its splendour tomorrow,' he said. 'You'll love it.'

Josie let herself drink in the most amazing view she had ever seen. Leon's arm was round her shoulder, holding her safely, and she thought that this was a moment she would remember all her life.

A distant tinkling sound made her turn around and look upwards at the mountain behind her. She had left her hat in the car, and she had to shield her eyes from the dazzling sun and the intense blue of the sky. The wild craggy beauty of the scenery struck her even more forcibly than the elegant coastline panorama below. Beyond the village, a little winding path led up to the ruins of what must have been an old medieval castle. She thought she remembered Leon saying something during lunch about a Saracen fort being the earliest settlement at Ste-Agnès. And there was the tinkling again! This time she saw where it came from. High up, beyond the ruins, she could just pick out three or four white goats, ambling easily amongst the scrubby bushes which clung to the rock face, the different notes of the bells round their necks wafting gently on the still air. It was just like something from a romantic travel film. 'Oh, how simply perfect,' she said.

Leon smiled. 'Somehow I thought it would be this side of the view that would appeal to you most,' he said. 'You see why they call Ste-Agnès an eagle's nest.'

Josie could have stayed for hours, just drinking in the view and delighting in the feel of Leon's arm holding her. But at last he said, 'There are lots of things to see—the ancient castle and the medieval garden where they hold concerts and plays—but we shan't have time now. We've got things to do in Menton.'

They walked back to the car, noticing that the other cars had gone, and Josie prepared herself for the downhill drive back to Menton. But if the drive up the long, steep hill had been something of a nightmare, going down was like a beautiful dream.

Leon pushed up the dividing arm of the seat and drew her close to him, and she let her head rest on his shoulder. Every now and then he took a hand briefly from the wheel to pat her arm and say, 'OK?' and she murmured, 'Fine, thanks.' She enjoyed the curves and bends, which Leon took so smoothly, each one making her lean even closer to his hard body. When, finally, the road flattened out and they were approaching Menton, Josie drew away from Leon and sat up and pulled her hat on, tucking her disordered curls underneath.

Leon found a free space in a quiet car park and switched off the engine. He turned to Josie. 'That wasn't so bad, was it?'

She looked up at him, her eyes shining. 'It was a marvellous experience,' she said. 'Thank you for taking me. I can't tell you how much I enjoyed it.'

He leaned towards her and tipped back the brim of her hat. 'Then show me,' he said softly.

She didn't know which of them started the kiss, only that it went on and on and she was transported into a bliss that she had never known before. When Leon at last drew away she felt she was almost going to faint. She looked up at him, not knowing what she expected him to say—make some sort of declaration of love, perhaps. She had put her whole heart into that kiss, and surely he must feel the strength of the bond between them.

But he said, in a voice full of amusement, 'Well, now I know.'

'Know what?' she asked. This wasn't going right.

'Just that you don't need any practice either,' he said with his teasing laugh.

Disappointment was like a lead weight. The afternoon had been a game to him—the silly pretence of being in love. It was a game in which you were liable to get hurt if you made the mistake of forgetting it was a game. She wouldn't make that mistake again.

She smiled brilliantly at him as he handed her out of the car. 'I'm glad you're convinced. I must be a good actress.'

He shrugged, as if he were no longer interested in the conversation, and closed the car door with a sharp slam. 'Now, let's get along to the bank,' he said, and set off down the road.

With a heavy heart, and a mind in confusion, Josie followed him.

CHAPTER SEVEN

THE bank was in one of the roads overlooking the
wide flowerbed which Josie had seen from the promenade. But even the fragrant scent of the hundreds of
rose bushes didn't invade her senses as it had done
before. She was still in a wretched state of muddle
when a clerk ushered her and Leon into the manager's
room, and she had to pull herself together and explain
that she wished to have an account opened.

Fortunately the manager spoke fluent English, and
was pleasant and helpful. When Leon had introduced
her, and she had explained her business and given the
manager the particulars he required, he asked her if
she intended to live permanently in Menton. Without
a glance at Leon she replied, 'Oh, yes. I've quite
fallen in love with the place. I certainly don't intend
to go back to London...'

The manager nodded sympathetically and said that
he, too, had decided to settle here when he retired, in
five years' time. He chatted for a few minutes with
Leon, said goodbye amiably and summoned a clerk
to take Josie to a counter where she could exchange
all her traveller's cheques for francs.

As they left the bank again, Leon seemed quite un-
aware of any change in Josie's mood. 'That went off
satisfactorily,' he said. 'Now we'll call at the jewellers; it's only round the corner.' Already he was

searching in his pocket for the ring-box. 'I want you to choose a ring you like.'

Josie didn't reply, but outside the small jeweller's shop in a side-road she hung back. 'I don't want to choose a ring,' she said. 'If we are going on with this silly pretence you should choose it yourself—something you like and can give to the girl you really want to marry.'

Leon looked hard at her, but her large hat was pulled down to cover her eyes. He shrugged. 'OK, if that's the way you want it,' he said in a resigned tone. 'Wait here for me, then.' He went into the shop.

Josie paced up and down, keeping her eyes averted from the trays of rings displayed in the shop window. After that kiss Leon had taken care to remind her that they were merely playing a game, and she wouldn't forget that again. She had read too much into the kiss, but then, she reminded herself, he must be experienced in the art of flirtation, which she certainly wasn't. She'd never had the time or opportunity. The fumbling kisses from the older boys at school and the goodnight kisses from Roger Ward when he drove her home from college were all she had to compare with Leon's kiss, and she knew now that it had marked the beginning of her growing up. The romantic love she had cherished for Roger had been just that—romantic—and she assured herself that what she had taken as love for Leon had been the same—romantic, not real.

A small, cynical smile played round her mouth. Dreams were part of growing up, and she ought to be past the age of dreams.

Leon emerged from the jeweller's shop, smiling and patting his pocket. Josie joined him, and they began to walk towards the spot where the car was parked.

It wasn't until they were driving up the hill to the villa that she said coolly, 'You found a ring you liked?'

'Yes, indeed. It just fits the bill—not at all flashy. I think you'll like it.'

'That doesn't really matter, as I'll be wearing it for only a few days.' She changed the subject quickly. 'Did your solicitor say exactly when Charles is likely to see the books and clear up the question of ownership of Mon Abri?'

He kept his eyes on the road. 'Are you so anxious to get rid of me?'

'Oh, it's not like that,' she said, taking the teasing question seriously. 'It's just that I'm looking forward to beginning my plans for my house.'

'I see,' he said with equal seriousness. 'Well, tomorrow I intend to begin on *my* plans for renovating the whole villa, and you promised to help me with some of the design work, you remember?'

She bit her lip. She had forgotten, but she wouldn't admit it. 'Of course. As you said, it will be good practice for me.'

Back at the villa, Josie went straight to the utility room to unload the washing machine. She hung the clean clothes on a line which had been put up to stretch the length of the room. They would all be dry by morning.

Just as she was finishing she heard Leon come into

the room. 'I've put drinks out on the terrace,' he said. 'It's not too hot out there.'

She shook out the last dress and hung it carefully over the line. 'I'll be with you in five minutes,' she said over her shoulder. When she turned round he had gone. There was a distinct change in the atmosphere, a certain coolness between them. She supposed it was safer than his playful intimacy, but she couldn't help thinking of his kindness and understanding during that frightening drive up the mountain. That, at least, had been real.

She had the keys of Mon Abri in her bag, and she went along to the front door and upstairs to her bedroom, tossed her hat on the bed and pulled a comb through her curls. In the shower-room she washed her hands and face. She felt suddenly very tired.

When she joined Leon on the terrace he looked hard at her. 'My poor Josie, you're worn out. All this rushing up and down mountains has been too much for you. Have a sip of sherry and then you must go upstairs and have a rest. I shall get supper tonight. I'm quite capable now you've taken the bandage off.'

'I'm OK,' she said. 'I can…'

He put a glass of sherry in her hand. 'Do as you're told,' he said sternly.

She swallowed a gulp of sherry and put the glass down.

'That's a good girl.' He patted her shoulder, then took her firmly by the arm and led her along the terrace, taking out his duplicate key to unlock the French window of Mon Abri. 'Now—off you go. I don't want to hear another squeak out of you until I call up to tell you supper's ready.'

Josie went slowly upstairs to her bedroom, lay down on the unmade bed and stared at the ceiling. When Leon was kind and thoughtful, when she heard something in his voice that seemed like tenderness, it was difficult to stop herself from indulging in the old dream. But stop she must. The situation was complicated enough as it was, without complicating it further. Why did Charles have to rush off to America and put himself out of reach? If he had been around to straighten out the ownership of Mon Abri, there wouldn't have been this week when she and Leon... No, she wouldn't think about it. Resolutely she closed her eyes and willed herself to relax.

She had fallen into a light sleep when she heard Leon calling her from downstairs. At the sound of his voice her heart lurched, and she was awake immediately and sat up. 'Coming,' she called back.

They had supper in the kitchen. Leon had prepared a colourful prawn salad, with nectarines and ice cream to follow. 'Is it enough?' he asked a little anxiously. 'I thought something cold would be OK as we had quite a substantial lunch.'

Josie hadn't the remotest memory of what she had had for lunch at Ste-Agnès. Her stomach hadn't settled down after that terrifying drive up the mountain. But she let that pass and said, 'This is delightful. Just right for a warm evening.'

'Good!' He pushed the salad bowl towards her for her to help herself. He apologised for the bread, which had been bought yesterday and was hard, but Josie said she was managing it quite well.

All the ease that had been building between them had gone. They were stiffly polite and might have been strangers, meeting for the first time. Well, they were indeed strangers, Josie thought. She knew nothing about Leon except that he wanted the villa complete, for his family, and he had seemed urgent about it. He had had every opportunity to tell her more, but he hadn't chosen to. Perhaps if they were working together tomorrow, he would explain further. Meanwhile she knew that she missed his light banter. Even their quarrelling had been better than this studied politeness.

Supper was a silent meal. Josie was thankful to retire to the terrace afterwards, while Leon made coffee. When he brought out the tray he said, 'I hope that's how you like it—about one-third milk.'

She produced a bright smile. 'Perfect, thank you.'

'Brandy?' He lifted the bottle. 'Sorry I haven't any other liqueurs.'

She shook her head. 'No brandy, thank you.' She drank the tepid coffee quickly, and glanced at her watch. 'If you'll excuse me, I'll say goodnight. I've got some tidying to do in my bedroom.' She got to her feet.

Leon stood up, putting down the brandy bottle. 'Before you go, I'd like you to see the ring I've bought and give me your professional opinion on the design.' He took the box from his pocket and lifted out the ring, holding it between finger and thumb for her inspection.

Josie had been hoping Leon had forgotten about the ring tonight, but he had put it in such a way that she couldn't refuse. She looked down at the ring. It was a square emerald set in a fascinating design of diamond chips. Leon's choice, then, and she loved it, but when he lifted her hand she drew it away quickly. 'I'll put it on myself, thanks.' If she let him put the ring on her finger he might make it an opportunity for kissing her again, and if he did she would not trust herself not to throw her arms round his neck and kiss him back. She had made a fool of herself once today, and she wasn't going to invite his laughing comment again.

He tossed the ring down on the table carelessly. 'What the hell's going on, Josie?' She heard the anger in his voice, and when she raised her head to look at him saw the steely gleam in the grey eyes fixed on her own.

'I—I don't know what you mean,' she faltered.

'You damn well do. We were getting along well together until suddenly, this afternoon, you froze up.' He added more gently, 'What is it, Josie? Can't you trust me?'

What would he say if she told him it was herself she couldn't trust? She improvised feebly, 'I think that all of a sudden I realised what this must be costing you. When I said I wanted a flashy ring I never dreamed that you would buy a genuine one. I feel guilty about it and wish I'd never agreed to this silly pretence of being engaged.'

'Oh, don't worry about that. When our little charade is over I shall keep the ring. I'm sure it will come in useful one day. I hope that salves your conscience?'

'I suppose so,' she said, not very graciously. It wasn't her conscience that was troubling her, but the thought of Leon tenderly putting the ring on to the finger of some unknown girl. But she must go on with the charade. She picked up the ring and pushed it on the third finger of her left hand, holding up her arm to examine it. 'Yes, I like it. It's very unusual and well designed.'

'Good, that's what I hoped you'd say. No qualms about wearing it now?'

That was not the way she would describe her feelings about the ring, but she shook her head and said, 'May I have the box, please? I must have somewhere safe to put the ring when I'm not wearing it. I shan't need it until tomorrow evening, to show off to Caroline.'

He frowned, but handed the box to her, and she took off the ring and carefully replaced it.

Still frowning, Leon said, 'I'd prefer you to wear it all the time. I want you to get used to the idea of our engagement before tomorrow evening.'

She raised her brows. '*You'd* prefer? *You* want?'

She met his eyes for what seemed several minutes. Then he burst out laughing. 'You're a bonny wee fighter, Josie Dunn.'

She didn't smile. 'Haven't you noticed that I don't take orders except when it suits me?'

He was still laughing. 'What a delightfully feminine attitude.'

'Well, I *am* female,' she retorted. 'How would a male express the same sentiment?'

'Do you really want me to tell you?' he said, his eyes twinkling. 'I have a wide vocabulary.'

'No,' Josie squeaked. Then she had to laugh herself. She might have known that the argument would go Leon's way.

He smiled his most charming smile at her. 'I should be very grateful if you would wear it all the time,' he said. 'Please, Josie.'

'That's more like it,' she said, putting the ring on her finger again.

The box had fallen on the floor, and she bent to pick it up. He bent at the same moment and their heads bumped together. Josie lost her balance and toppled sideways on to the tiled floor. Leon held out his hands to help her up, keeping one arm round her waist and giving her a hug. 'Friends again, Josie?'

His head was getting closer, and she knew he was going to kiss her. What had he said the last time they had declared their friendship? 'Friends may kiss'? But not this time, Mr Leon Kent. She wriggled away from him, laughing. 'Yes, friends again, if that's what you want.' She held out her hand and he took it in a hard grip.

'I certainly do want it,' he said, 'for the moment.' His look was enigmatic, but she pretended not to notice it.

'Now I'm really going up to tidy my room. Goodnight, Leon.'

'Goodnight, Josie. Let me know if you need help.'

'Thanks, I will,' she said, vowing that however aw-

ful the difficulties of taking possession of Mon Abri
were she would cope with them herself this time, and
not go running to him for help.

It was swelteringly hot upstairs, and the cream
dress was sticking to her. She pulled off her sandals
and then stripped her clothes off. She was longing for
a shower. But when she looked at the various taps on
the antiquated shower she knew she couldn't remember what Gaston had explained about working them.
She wouldn't go to Leon for help, so had to be content
with swilling her face and sluicing the rest of her body
with water in her cupped hands. There was a pool of
water on the floor when she had finished, but it hardly
seemed to matter if it went through to the ceiling of
the sitting-room below. There were no towels except
one small hand-towel, and she patted herself with that.
She would soon dry in this heat.

Back in the bedroom, she sank down on the bed.
She stared at the ring which she had laid on the chest
of drawers. She would wear it for possibly five days,
until Charles came back to clear up the ownership of
Mon Abri. Then she would give it back to Leon, who
would, in due course, put it on the finger of the girl
he wanted to marry. Tears pricked behind her eyes,
but she blinked them away impatiently. Just because
she had fallen in love with him it didn't follow that
he felt the same about her. Again she thought that
pretending to be in love when you really were in love
was the hardest thing a girl could be expected to do.

She remembered how Leon had said, 'For God's
sake forget about attitudes. Just be yourself.' Right,
she would be herself, the practical, realistic self. No

more dreams. No more misery. She was having a lovely holiday, seeing all sorts of exciting new places, and tomorrow she would see the famous Monte Carlo. She would take each day as it came, and not swoon if Leon gave her a playful kiss. 'Friends may kiss', he had said, and that was the modern way. A few kisses didn't mean an engagement ring.

Oh, dear, how naive and childish she had been. Never mind, it would all be different, easier, from now on.

Josie put on the lightest nightie she possessed, lay down and, on this encouraging resolution, fell asleep.

She wakened early, hurriedly dressed in shorts and the only clean T-shirt she had left, pushed her curls into place, swilled her face and hands and ran downstairs, letting out a gasp as she nearly fell over Leon at the bottom. He was on his hands and knees, crawling across the floor, and he seemed to be holding his breath.

She sat down on the third step from the bottom. 'Good morning, Leon,' she said brightly. 'What on earth are you doing there?'

He did not reply, but went on cautiously crawling towards the wall on the far side of the room. Then she saw that he held a small flat case in his hand, from which he was paying out a length of steel measuring tape, the end of which was secured at the opposite wall. He had about another yard to go when suddenly the end of the tape sprang loose and began to wind itself back. Leon let out his breath, then a string of words, most of which were unfamiliar to

Josie. She wasn't listening. She grabbed the end of
the tape as it passed her and examined it. A metal
tape would have a hook at the end to attach it to some
suitable object. This tape had no hook. She let go of
it and it slowly reeled itself back into its case.

Leon sat back on his heels, and looked up at her as
if he were seeing her for the first time. 'I've been
wrestling with that damned thing for an hour or more.
Some idiot at the London office must have packed the
wrong tape. This one's broken. Sorry about the language,' he added.

She didn't waste time on inessentials. 'Tell me
what you want to measure,' she said in a businesslike
voice, 'and I'll stand on the end of the tape.'

'Thanks,' he said briefly, and explained to her. A
couple of minutes later Leon had the measurement he
wanted and had jotted it down on the pad beside him
on the floor.

He let out a long breath. 'You arrived just in time
to save my sanity. I must have the measurements in
here before I can draw up my first—before I can begin
to work out my ideas.'

Josie nodded casually. 'Have you had breakfast?'
she said.

He stood up, brushing the dust from his jeans. 'Is
that your way of reminding me that I don't own Mon
Abri yet, and that it's infernal cheek to be coming in
here without permission?'

Josie laughed. 'What a suspicious mind you have!
I simply meant that I want breakfast even if you
don't.' She walked to the door. 'And I expect you

will own Mon Abri before long. You seem to get just what you want. I'll make some coffee.'

She couldn't wait to enjoy the expression on his face, and walked straight along to the next-door kitchen. Here she set the coffee machine to work, and was delighted to notice that there were newly-baked baguettes and a packet of croissants on the worktop. They smelled delicious. Leon came in and stood looking doubtfully at her, but before he could speak she said, 'How clever of you to get these. Did you get up at the crack of dawn?'

'I remembered that there was a house just down the road where Madame makes bread each day. It's mostly for the local golf club, but if you wheedle her nicely she'll usually oblige.'

'See what I mean?' Josie smiled, putting butter and jam on the table.

No,' he said. 'What?'

'That you get what you want—by wheedling if necessary. You won't be able to wheedle Charles, if he finds that Mon Abri belongs to me.'

'No,' said Leon thoughtfully, and when he looked at her there were little devils dancing in his eyes. 'But I could always wheedle you.'

'Never,' she declared stoutly, her own eyes dancing as they met his. They laughed together, and she felt a warm surge of happiness. They were friends again, and that was how she meant to keep it.

Leon had his breakfast standing up, and as soon as he had finished disappeared into the sitting-room with a word of apology. She saw a different side of him today. This was his job and he couldn't wait to get on with it. He was the professional.

Josie took her time, and when she had washed up she went through to join him.

The table was in the middle of the room, and on it was a drawing board with a sheet of paper clipped to it. More pads of paper leaned against the table leg, together with Leon's briefcase. On the edge of the table was a box containing drawing instruments which reminded Josie of her school days—a set-square, a protractor, a ruler.

'You see what I'm doing?' he said as she came up beside him. 'Now I've got the measurements of Mon Abri I can make a rough sketch of the whole ground floor as it will be.' He pointed with the gold pencil he was holding. 'This part is the present room, and this is Mon Abri just as it is. Of course the kitchen will come out, and the stairs.' He drew his pencil through the indication of both on the plan. 'And the front door won't be necessary. Then, if the dividing wall between the two houses is taken down...' He scribbled through the line which indicated the wall.

Josie watched the gold pencil heartlessly disposing of her little house bit by bit, and foolishly her eyes swam with tears. She sniffed, and fumbled for a handkerchief. Leon looked up. 'What's wrong, Josie?'

She pulled out her handkerchief from the belt of her shorts and blew her nose. 'Nothing,' she said feebly.

'Come on, you might as well tell me. I shall get it out of you sooner or later.'

'Don't bully me.' She blinked away the tears.

He waited, tapping his pencil on the board.

'OK, I'll tell you. Mon Abri means a lot to me. Ever since my solicitor told me I'd inherited a house in France I've dreamed about it, planned it in my mind. It was the best thing that ever happened. And then—when I got here—everything went wrong, right from the start. And now, watching you cross it all out, it's like seeing it pulled down before my eyes. Now go on—laugh.' She sniffed again.

'I'm not laughing,' he said. He shook his head slowly. 'Oh, Josie, Josie, and you once told me you weren't romantic. Do you still want Mon Abri as much as that?'

'Yes—no—I don't know. The fun seems to have gone out of it.'

'Is that my doing?'

She pulled a face at him. 'Well, you weren't very welcoming at first, but afterwards you couldn't have been more helpful.'

He put down his pencil, stood up and, taking her hand, led her to the big sofa and drew her down beside him. 'You're a puzzle to me, Josie. You're twenty-three and yet sometimes you seem so much younger. Have you had what used to be called "a sheltered life"?'

She considered that. 'I suppose I have. I was just sixteen when my parents were divorced. I was going to go away to an art college to study design, but my mother had a sort of nervous breakdown and I couldn't leave home. She relied on me for everything. There was nobody else, you see. And if I went out to an evening class at the local college, I often got home to find her in a state of collapse. She recovered a little, but she was always ill with one thing or another. I looked after her and the home until she died of pneumonia last Christmas.' She realised that he was still holding her hand, and gently pulled it away.

He frowned slightly. 'No parties? No boyfriends?'

'No. My mother was terrified that if I went out with anyone I'd get married and leave her.' She sighed. 'My love-life consists of a passion I had for one of the professors at college, who gave me a lift home. Then I found out he was married, so that was that.'

'Poor little Josie,' he said softly. 'So that silver-framed photograph...?'

'Yes, that's a picture of my mother. Oh, I wasn't unhappy,' she added quickly. 'I loved her very much and I was too busy to be sorry for myself.' She sat up, smiling. 'And now you have the story of my life. Though why you should want it I don't know. And, as I'm sure you don't want to tell me yours, let's get on with the plan.'

She got up and pulled another chair to the table. Leon followed slowly. 'I'll tell you what we'll do,' he said. 'We'll leave my plan for the time being and make a plan for Mon Abri. Work out what you will have to do if you decide to keep it. How does that strike you?'

'Fine,' she said. He really was being very kind and understanding.

He secured a piece of detail paper on top of the first one and on this he drew an outline of Mon Abri, copied from the plan underneath. It looked very small.

'I think the best thing to do would be to build a

wing at the side for the kitchen and utility room.' He drew it in quickly. 'Of course I'd like to do the design by computer. You don't happen to have a digital computer with you, do you?'

''Fraid not,' Josie giggled. She was enjoying this morning after all.

There wasn't very much that could be done to improve the little house, and when he had finished Leon tore off the sheet and handed it to Josie. 'There you are,' he said. 'Keep it for possible future use.'

'Thanks, I will.' She folded up the sheet.

He put in a fresh sheet of detail paper and went back to his original work. Watching him, Josie didn't wince this time when he reduced Mon Abri to a shell. He talked to himself as he worked. 'We have one, two, three, four, five bedrooms now, and we shall need six...' He bit his lip. 'One on the ground floor, of course, with shower-room—here.' And he pencilled it in.

Josie longed to ask him about his family. There must be a large number of them to need all those bedrooms. But she held back, although he hadn't hesitated to ask her about her upbringing. She would have to wait until he told her—if he ever did.

Leon looked round at her. 'I thought you were going to do some designing for the new house,' he said.

'Oh, not for the new house. You can't do any designing for rooms unless you know the people who are going to use them.'

'No, I suppose not.' He looked suddenly withdrawn. His hands rested on the table. 'Well, that would take too long, so why not limit your ideas to Mon Abri?'

She shook her head, aware of disappointment that he hadn't been more forthcoming about his family. 'No, I think I'll leave that until later.' She pushed back her chair. 'I won't interrupt you any more,' she said, and went back to the kitchen before he could reply.

In the utility room, all her clothes were dry. She folded them and carried them up to her bedroom next door. Here she collected the cream dress and lacy pants she had worn yesterday, and took them back to the utility room to wash by hand. As she went through the routine tasks her mind was far away.

Far away with Leon and his family, and why he wouldn't speak of them but seemed to need above everything to have this house for them.

As she walked back she could see through the kitchen straight into the sitting-room. Leon was sitting at the drawing-board, but he wasn't adding to his plan. He was sitting with his elbows on the table and his head in his hands, the picture of unhappiness. She lingered, her heart going out to him in his trouble, whatever it was, and wished that she could help him. She could, of course. She could renounce any claim she might have to Mon Abri, if it turned out to be really hers, and then Leon would be happy again.

There and then she made up her mind. She couldn't wait for Charles to come home.

Josie hurried along to the kitchen, making a clatter with mugs for coffee, giving him time to pull himself together. When she went into the sitting-room he was sitting up again, and she saw that the drawing-board was no longer on the table.

'I've given up for the time being,' he said. 'I have all the measurements, and I can do the job properly when I have my computer.' He glanced up at her. 'And, of course, when I know that the house is mine.'

'It shouldn't be long now,' Josie said, wishing she could tell him what she had decided and see the look of relief on his face. But she couldn't give up Mon Abri until she knew she really owned it.

'I came to see if you would like coffee,' she said.

'I should, very much, thanks,' he said absently.

When she returned with a tray of coffee he had moved to the sofa and drawn up a small table. He stood up and took the tray from her, putting it on the table. Then he patted the seat beside him. 'Come and sit down and we can have a good moan together.'

She sat down. 'What about?' she queried. 'I never allow myself to moan much.'

'Don't you find these days of waiting somewhat trying?'

She said lightly, 'Not really. I've only been here three days, and they certainly haven't been uneventful. And Charles must be back very soon, then all our troubles will be over.'

He said moodily, 'Will they?'

Josie jumped when a buzzing noise came from the direction of a table beside the window.

Leon was on his feet immediately. 'The phone, at last.' He crossed the room in two strides and picked up the receiver. *'Allo? Bonjour—oui—bon—très bien—merci, au revoir.'* He replaced the receiver and looked round at Josie. 'All systems go—I'll ring up London and find out if they have any news.'

He began to dial. Josie went into the kitchen and closed the door behind her. She could hear Leon's voice, but not what he said.

Presently he came bursting in, his moodiness dispelled. 'You needn't have been tactful,' he said. 'This concerns both of us.' He took her hand and led her back to the sitting-room. 'Sit down and finish your coffee.' He drained his own cup as they sat together again on the sofa. 'I got through to Charles's secretary. It seems that he is returning to London today and will be in touch as soon as he has sorted out the difficulty. So we won't need to moan after all.' He put an arm round her waist and hugged her. 'Good news at last!'

It wasn't good news to Josie. She didn't want these days with Leon to end. But when he knew he had the whole house to plan for she wouldn't be necessary in his life and she wouldn't see him again. She felt empty inside, and took a gulp of coffee. 'What will you do if you find you haven't got Mon Abri?' she asked him in a small voice.

He frowned. 'If Charles has let me down over this, he'll damn well have to find me another place as large as this one pretty quickly. And that's not going to be easy,' he added, grey eyes brooding.

'No,' she said. 'I suppose not. It wouldn't be very easy for me to give up Mon Abri either. I'd have to find somewhere else down here. I've grown rather fond of Menton.'

She thought he brightened. 'We could have a good

look round,' he said. 'There must be some place you'd like.'

She wrinkled her nose. 'A flat, probably, like I had in London, with no view.'

'Oh, no, we'd find somewhere better than that for you. A nice little house, perhaps. Oh, well, don't let's talk about it. Let's wait and see.'

His arm was still round her waist. She could feel the warmth of his hand through the thin stuff of her shirt. She wanted urgently to move closer to him, to put her head on his shoulder. As if he had read her thought the pressure of his hand increased, but she wriggled away and stood up. 'I've got some ironing to do,' she said. 'I'll go and see if I can find an iron in the utility room. And I want to give my new dress a look over. Is it suitable to wear tonight in Monte Carlo, do you think?'

'Perfectly,' he said. 'I shall be proud of you. I'm glad you're wearing my ring. The green almost matches your eyes when you're angry.' He picked up her left hand and held it to his cheek for a moment. 'Now, run along and get your ironing done before lunch. I'm going down to the town; I've got one or two things to do. I'll bring back something for lunch from the supermarket.'

'Could you possibly bring me back a towel?' she asked him. 'There aren't any here.'

'I will,' he said, and went to the door. 'See you later.'

Josie stood where he had left her, a rueful little smile round her mouth. Such a domestic little

exchange! Just as if they were a married couple!
Instead of which they were 'just friends'.

She had to remember that when she was pretending
to be engaged to him this evening.

She resolved to remind herself all the way to Monte
Carlo. And when they were there—

Well, that would have to look after itself.

CHAPTER EIGHT

THE fluted skirt of the yellow dress floated out as Josie twirled round before the long mirror in Leon's spare bedroom. He had offered the room for her to dress for the evening ahead in such a friendly way that she couldn't refuse. 'I'll dress first, and then you can have the place to yourself and we'll meet at half past eight, shall we?' She had accepted gratefully. She hadn't yet mastered the workings of the shower in her own house, and she was determined not to fly to Leon for help once again. Also, the only looking-glass in her bedroom was pathetically small, and she couldn't have enjoyed the pleasure of seeing the skirt of the yellow dress slide over her head and mould itself over her hips until it fell gracefully to end just below her knees.

It really was a lovely dress. She'd never bought a dress on the spur of the moment like that, without even enquiring about the price. She must have gone slightly mad, she thought now. Or had it been because Leon was with her? Whatever the reason, it had turned out well.

But she surveyed herself a little doubtfully when she'd carefully guided the top over her head. It was cut dangerously low at the front, and lower still at the back. It hung loose to rest on her hips and Josie wasn't quite sure that it would stay in place without

127

slipping off her shoulder. But the cut was too clever for that, and, having turned and twisted several times, she was reassured.

She glanced at her watch. Nearly half past eight. Her mother had given her a single string of pearls for a twenty-first birthday present, and now she clasped it round her neck, checked that she was wearing the emerald ring, draped the chiffon scarf round her shoulders, pulled on white sandals, picked up her small handbag and ran down the stairs.

Leon was waiting for her on the terrace, looking so handsome in his white tuxedo that her heart missed a beat.

'Right on time,' he said. She saw the gleam in his eyes as he surveyed what the scarf did not hide, but all he said was, 'You made a good choice. That dress is just right for a warm evening.' Josie glanced quickly at his face, suspecting that he was teasing her, but he smiled innocently as he added, 'And it's a pretty dress for a pretty young lady.'

She dropped a mock curtsy. 'Thank you, sir.' Just friends, she reminded herself, and thought that the evening was getting off to a good start.

It continued like that as Leon drove slowly along the winding coast road to Monte Carlo, allowing time to point out the various small villages nestling around the larger coves and inlets on the way. The sun was disappearing behind the mountains on their right, leaving a sky suffused with colour. With delight, Josie silently tried to memorise the exact shades of coral and gold, amber and peach and pale apple-green.

'Designing a cushion cover?' Leon enquired, with a quick glance at her rapt face.

He always seemed to know what she was thinking. It was dangerous.

'Um, sort of,' she said vaguely.

Leon chuckled. 'The sunsets are always in competition with Monte Carlo's lights. You won't see much colour there. So look your fill.'

She sighed. 'It's glorious, isn't it?'

'Glorious,' he echoed softly, with a glance over his shoulder at her face. She felt her cheeks grow hot, and couldn't think of a retort.

A couple of minutes later, Leon said, 'Well, here we are. We go through a tunnel first, which brings us out near the Casino. Monte Carlo is short of building space, and they have to build upwards in high-rise flats or downwards into tunnels.'

The first thing that Josie saw when they emerged from the tunnel was a blaze of light everywhere. 'The Casino's over there.' Leon waved a hand. 'We're meeting Caroline and friend on the steps. Would you like to be dropped off there, or will you come with me to park the car?'

'I'll come with you, please,' Josie said hastily. She knew it was silly to be nervous, but she felt as if she were acting in a play and didn't know her lines.

Leon drove on to an underground car park, which was only half full. When Josie remarked about this, he said, 'Oh, the serious gambling doesn't start in Monte Carlo until about now, and goes on all night.'

'We shan't stay all night?' Josie was rather horrified.

'Not unless you want to leave all your money in the gaming rooms.' Leon smiled. He came round to open her door. She slid out, but instead of giving her his hand he put an arm round her waist and drew her towards him.

Just friends, Josie reminded herself, twisting away.

He pulled her back strongly. 'What's all this?' Although she couldn't see his face in the dim light she guessed that he had his teasing smile. 'Have you forgotten? We're going to be married.'

She managed to keep her voice light as she retorted, 'This year, next year, some time, never.'

Leon held her more tightly. 'Who was it said, "Never say never"?' His deep voice sounded close to her ear.

'I don't know,' Josie muttered.

'Well, I'm saying it now. *Never* say never.' He lowered his head and kissed her mouth, a swift kiss, demanding no response from her. 'That's just to remind you—for tonight.'

Just for tonight, Josie thought, and her nervous flutters subsided. She knew her part now, and she would play it to the best of her ability. Just for tonight, she decided, looking up at Leon's dark face as they walked together towards the Casino, I'll let myself dream and then it will come easily.

She soon recognised the Casino as Leon said, 'It always reminds me of an iced wedding cake.'

They were in an open area before the fabulous building now. To the side a profusion of flowers grew in immaculate lawns divided by stretches of water where water-lilies had folded their petals for the night.

Bordering the Casino itself, paths ran gently upwards among exotic-looking shrubs and trees. Nothing had been spared to present the Casino as a breathtaking marvel of architecture. Josie stood still and gazed at it, fascinated. She had seen small photographs of it in her guide book but the reality was amazing. Her eyes moved up the gleaming façade, floodlit from below, past the great first-floor windows and the statues of elegant sea-gods holding their tridents, to pause at the unbelievably ornate roofline with its filigree corner towers and bronze angels sprawling seductively on either side of an ornate clock.

'I see what you mean about a wedding cake,' said Josie, 'but this is like a wedding cake from a grand opera.'

'Spoken like a true romantic,' Leon replied. 'You know it was designed by Charles Garnier, the architect of the Paris Opéra? And it's even more fantastic inside, I can assure you. But don't forget it's really all about making money—or losing it. Ah, here's Caroline now.'

A girl in a very short scarlet dress came running down the steps in front of the casino, threading her way between the strolling groups, waving gaily. 'Hi, Leon.' She greeted him with a kiss and then turned to look at Josie. 'You came along too, then. You're still shacking up with Leon, are you?' Her lips curled.

Leon's arm went round Josie's shoulder. 'That's an extremely ill-mannered remark, Caroline. Josie and I are going to be married. I think you should apologise.'

'Married?' drawled Caroline. 'How nice! My mistake, then.'

'You'll have to do better than that.' Leon's arm tightened round Josie's shoulders, as if to reassure her.

'I agree entirely.' A man's voice cut in. 'Perhaps I may apologise in her place.'

He came forward, giving a little bow towards Josie. 'I'm ashamed of you, Caro.'

'Who asked you to butt in?' Caroline said sulkily.

'It was necessary, until you learn some manners,' the young man said suavely. He was tall and thin, with a handsome, intelligent face, and he spoke English with a slight French accent. 'And now I think you had better introduce me to your friends.'

Caroline glared at him and muttered, 'This is Jean-Claude. Leon Kent and...' She trailed off, pretending not to remember Josie's name.

Leon shook hands with the tall Frenchman, saying, 'This is Josie Dunn, my fiancée.'

Josie's hand was held in a firm grasp. 'May I wish you both happiness?' the young man said formally.

The Frenchman was a peacemaker. 'We all know each other now, so how about finding something to eat?'

Caroline clapped her hands. 'Yes, let's. I'm starving. We'll go to that place on La Condamine we found last week.'

Jean-Claude looked at the other two. 'Is that agreeable? It's not far to walk, or shall I get my car?'

'I'd love to walk,' Josie said. A walk might blow away the nasty atmosphere left behind by Caroline's rudeness.

Caroline linked her arm with Leon's. 'I want to hear all about what you've been doing in the last eight years,' she said brightly. She had got over her show of bad temper.

Leon raised an eyebrow towards Josie with a little shrug, and allowed Caroline to lead him off through the groups of strollers.

Josie looked up at Jean-Claude and saw the dark frown that disfigured his handsome face. She said impulsively, 'Please don't worry about my feelings being hurt. I know that Caroline doesn't like me. She showed it quite plainly when we met for the first time recently.'

The frown disappeared. 'It's generous of you to take her rudeness so well. I'm afraid she's in a bad mood—she's got some trouble at home. And she's very immature for her age. She resents competition.'

'Competition?'

He looked down into her face, 'It is difficult to explain without sounding too personal. Let us just say that she sees that you are the better looking and that you have a much more attractive dress.'

Josie looked ahead to where the other two were walking. Caroline had said that she wanted Leon to tell her all his news, but it seemed that she was doing the talking herself. She hung on to his arm, looking up at him eagerly as she spoke.

Josie's eyes twinkled up at the Frenchman as she said, 'The second I'll allow. The first—no. She's very lovely.'

He sighed. 'Yes, she is. The thing is that she lacks confidence, and acts badly when she imagines she's being outshone. I forgive her because I love her,' he added simply. 'But you understand all about that, do you not?'

Josie's eyes searched out Leon's dark head among the crowd. 'Oh, yes, yes, I do understand. It's not always easy.' A now familiar weakness ran through her, and her heart seemed to squeeze up as she lived again the moment when Leon had held her in his arms in the dimness of the car park, when he had whispered, 'Never say never.' If only he had meant it! If only she could be sure he wasn't using his charm to soften her will to oppose him about the ownership of the villa! Sometimes she had seen what she thought was tenderness in his grey eyes, and then he had made some teasing remark that spoilt it. 'Oh, yes, I do understand,' she said again.

Soon they left the crowded forecourt of the casino behind and were walking along quiet paths under palm trees, between semi-tropical plants with huge, shiny leaves and giant cactuses which sent out gaudy flowers. 'Where are we now?' Josie enquired. 'It's beautiful here, so cool and green, like walking under the sea.'

'The Casino Gardens,' Jean-Claude told her. 'They're quite famous.'

There were few people around here, and Leon and Caroline were only a short distance in front. They could easily have dropped back and joined up with us, Josie thought, but, although Leon glanced over his shoulder, Caroline seemed to be urging him to keep out of hearing distance.

'This is your first visit to our wicked city?' Jean-Claude asked.

Josie nodded. 'I've only been in the South of France once, when I was a child, and I'm having difficulty with the language. I thought I would be able to understand it, but Leon says the people in Menton speak a Provençal *patois* and it floors me completely. Are you from this part? You speak such very good English.'

'I was educated in England—school and university—but I'm a true Monegasque actually. My family has lived here for many years. My father owns one of the hotels—which is why I'm learning about hotel management, from all angles. He expects me to take on the managership fairly soon.'

'I see,' Josie said, grateful to him for keeping up a light conversation. 'And you're working at the same hotel as Caroline at present?'

'No, unfortunately for me,' he said. 'I work at the Casino, in the gaming rooms. Most hotels here have gaming rooms, and I need to know how they are run.'

'What do you do?'

He pulled a face. 'A most disgraceful job, I fear. I work as a croupier.'

She gave him a surprised look. 'I'm very ignorant. What is a croupier, and why is it so disgraceful?'

'I'm the man who rakes in the chips at the gaming tables,' Jean-Claude said, with a smile in his serious brown eyes.

Josie laughed. 'Oh, I see.'

They had come out of the gardens now, and were walking along a boulevard on the sea front under a row of palm trees. Pinpoints of light from boats showed here and there on the dark sea. The sky was still streaked with colours left by the sunset. Josie said, 'This may be a wicked city but it's very beautiful.'

Jean-Claude was obviously pleased. He told her a little about the history of the place, but she noticed that his eyes would go worriedly to rest on Caroline's gold head as she still held on to Leon's arm.

At last the two in front came to a halt outside a brightly lit restaurant and they all trooped upstairs. The room was crowded, but they managed to get a table overlooking what Leon told Josie was the port of Monte Carlo. He pulled out a chair for her and sat down beside her. 'Did you think I'd deserted you, sweetheart?' He leant close and planted a kiss under Josie's ear. 'This child is more of a chatterbox than when I last saw her eight years ago.'

Caroline pouted, but it was obvious that her mood had changed. She actually smiled across the table at Josie. 'Leon insists that I apologise,' she said, 'and I do. Will you forgive me for being so horrid?' She had an angelic smile, and Josie could understand why Jean-Claude had fallen in love with her.

'Of course I will,' Josie said. 'We all get cross sometimes. You should hear the things I say to Leon.' She grinned up at him and he squeezed her shoulders.

'All is forgiven,' he said.

'What a beautiful ring. May I look?' Caroline said.

Josie stretched her arm across the table for the ring to be admired. 'Look, Jean, isn't it super?'

Well, thought Josie, the ring seems to have served its purpose. And she must play her part—the part of a newly engaged girl, brimming over with happiness.

'I adore it,' she said, drawing her hand back and giving the ring a loving look. She rubbed her cheek against Leon's cheek. 'Such a generous darling, isn't he?'

He drew her very close and whispered, 'Well done!'

He couldn't resist reminding her that she was playing a part. But she remembered his voice when he had murmured, 'Never say never.' She had no way of understanding him and he didn't intend that she should.

The evening was more enjoyable than Josie would have thought possible. Monte Carlo seemed to invite you to be happy.

Jean-Claude took charge of the proceedings. He was so proud of being a true Monegasque that it was quite touching.

They all agreed that he should order the meal, and when that had been done Josie looked enquiringly across at him. 'Where are we now, exactly?' she asked.

'We are at the curve of the harbour, between two peaks of rock,' he told her. He lifted both hands, palms upwards.

'On my right, Monaco,' he intoned, in the voice of a tourist guide. 'You will see the medieval castle and the cathedral on the top of the rock. The castle has been added to over the years and is the residence of the Prince of Monaco and his family.' Josie gazed towards the fantastic building, with its wide frontage of columns and arches, floodlit and pure white against the blackness of the rock.

'On my left, Monte Carlo,' Jean-Claude went on. 'You will recognise the Casino, of course.' The lights were so dazzling that Josie could hardly recognise anything from this distance. It was all a glittering blur of light.

'And finally, the harbour below us.' Jean-Claude pointed down to where a pleasure boat was moving slowly across the dark water. Every small window shone with light and Josie exclaimed with pleasure, 'Oh, how lovely everything is!' She looked up at Leon. 'Can we come here again, darling? There's such a lot to be seen.'

'Of course we can,' Leon said with a grin. How easy it was to believe that the dream was coming true! Dangerous, but easy—and Josie didn't care. The lure of Monte Carlo must have got into her, she thought.

Dinner was a light-hearted affair. Jean-Claude had worked for a time in the kitchens of his father's hotel, he told them, and boasted that the meal he had ordered was a true Monegasque one. Josie hoped she would like it, and was relieved to find that she did. Jean-Claude even knew exactly how the main dish, *stocafi*, had been made, with small cubes of fish, onions and tomatoes, sautéed in olive oil, and special herbs in white wine, with black olives and cognac added. Leon approved of it, and asked Jean-Claude to write down the recipe. 'I shall expect you to cook it for me when we are married,' Leon told Josie. 'And don't forget the cognac.'

They lingered over the meal, laughing a lot and consuming a good deal of wine, chosen, of course, by Jean-Claude, and afterwards strolled back to the

Casino, the way they had come. Only this time Josie had Leon beside her. She leaned against him as he put his arm round her. She would remember this moment, she thought, in this lovely, shady place, with the smell of plants and flowers and the faint sound of a band playing in the distance.

'You seemed to be getting along well with Jean-Claude,' Leon said. 'What do you think of him?'

'Oh, I like him very much. He's so straightforward and—' she groped for a word '—so serious.'

There was a small silence. Then Leon said, 'You like serious men, do you?'

There was an odd note in his voice. He couldn't be jealous, could he? She passed a hand across her forehead, wondering how to reply and wishing she hadn't had that last glass of wine at dinner.

'Well—yes.'

'Hmm. I'll have to see what I can do.'

'Oh, I didn't mean…' she faltered.

'Don't worry, I know what you meant.'

He always knew what she meant, she thought, rather crossly, and she hardly ever knew what *he* meant. What a maddening man he was!

Jean-Claude and Caroline were waiting for them at the foot of the Casino steps. Caroline was looking blissfully happy now, and the way she stood close to Jean-Claude and looked up at him told its own story. He, too, looked quietly satisfied. They had evidently made up the disagreement of earlier in the evening.

'Come along, you two.' Jean-Claude led the way up the steps. 'You can't visit Monte Carlo without seeing the inside of the Casino.'

'Jean-Claude can show you round as he has a top job,' Caroline told them proudly.

Josie thought that the inside of the Casino was even grander than the outside. The first room they came to was enormous, decorated in crimson and gold, with frescoes and paintings round the walls and figures in glass cases dressed in period costumes. 'These are mostly characters from operas,' Jean-Claude said. 'They put operas and concerts and ballets on here. We're lucky that there's nothing going on tonight so that we can see inside. Now we'll go to the gaming rooms.'

He led them through a succession of rooms, the first being vast, with many tables. Roulette was the only game that Josie knew about, and there were several that she had never heard of—Black Jack, *Trente et Quarante*, *Punto Banco* and rows of automatic machines, whose clatter drowned the sound of the roulette wheel. Jean-Claude explained everything, and they lingered at the tables to watch the play.

What he called the private rooms were quieter rooms in succession, where the play was taken much more seriously. They moved from one to the next, just looking into each briefly, until the room at the end, where, they were told, it cost a hundred francs to play. It seemed to Josie that a great deal of money was changing hands, and the faces of the players round the tables were strained and anxious.

Josie was beginning to feel slightly overwhelmed by the size of the place, and was rather glad to get out into the open air again.

'Now what to do?' Jean-Claude wondered. 'Shall we go and have coffee?'

'Oh, yes,' Caroline agreed. 'Let's go to the Café de Paris—it's only just round the corner and *very* plushy.'

It was indeed plushy, Josie thought as they sat in the lounge. At another time she would have been making a mental note of the decoration of the luxurious room, but she was letting herself sink into a dream of happiness and her thoughts were all centred on Leon, sitting so close beside her on a cushioned banquette and looking so heartbreakingly handsome in his expertly tailored white jacket fitting smoothly over broad shoulders. His dark hair was a little out of place. She reached up and pushed a strand back, allowing her fingers to linger on his forehead, stroking it gently. She was playing her part well, she thought, and it was so easy now. He drew her hand down and kissed it, finger by finger. 'I'm enjoying being engaged,' he whispered.

She gave a little gurgle of laughter. 'I think I am, too.'

When Caroline said that they must go along to a disco next, Josie agreed gaily. The evening was taking on an air of unreality for her, and the disco, with its coloured strobe lights and ear-splitting music was part of the dream.

Caroline and Jean-Claude were on the floor already, bobbing up and down, and Josie thought, I've missed all the fun of being young. I've never been to discos or parties, or been one of a crowd of young people. But I'm living it up now, she thought, and she didn't know how brightly her hazel eyes shone in the changing lights.

Leon had to shout to make himself heard above the deafening noise of the speakers. He said, 'Are you an expert at this sort of thing?'

She shook her head. 'No,' was all she could make him understand. He took both her hands and they joined the couples on the crowded floor. It was easy to move to the beat of the music, and Leon still held her hands and moved opposite with the rhythmic, rather lazy grace of an athlete. When the music stopped at last they were joined by Caroline and Jean-Claude, and after a short interval they changed partners. Josie smiled brilliantly at the tall Frenchman, and hoped that Leon would notice. Jean-Claude was an expert, putting in fancy steps now and again. She guessed that his father's hotel had a disco and he had had to learn all about it in his rise to managership. She must remember to ask him.

When Leon claimed her again he muttered, 'To hell with this apartness,' and pulled her quite roughly into his arms. She melted against him willingly and they danced cheek to cheek, swaying to the beat while the coloured strobe lights passing over them seemed to be a perfect background to her dream.

It ended too soon for her. Leon broke away and led her off the floor. Outside the doors he said rather shortly, 'We'll go now. We have to drive home. Wait here a minute and I'll tell Caroline we're leaving.'

There was an outside door to the disco, and when Leon had collected the other two they said goodbye. Jean-Claude was thanked for his guided tour.

'You must come again,' he said. 'There's so much more to see.' He kissed Josie on both cheeks and shook hands with Leon, and Caroline impulsively kissed Josie, much to her surprise, before she put her arms round Leon's neck and kissed him too.

When the goodbyes were finally said, Josie walked in silence beside Leon to the darkened car park, now packed solidly with cars. He opened the door for her and waited for her to get in, not touching her to help her. The play was over, she thought sadly. It had been a lovely dream for just a few hours.

Leon still didn't speak as he backed the car out and drove slowly through the tunnel and out on to the Menton road. Josie turned to look out of the back window, but the lights were not visible from here. There was only the moonlight on the shadowy hills and the patches of silver where its light caught the tips of the waves. She laid her head back with a long sigh and closed her eyes.

There was a good deal of traffic on the road, but in a quiet spell Leon looked down at her. 'Poor child, has the effort of being engaged to me been too much for you?'

She sat up. 'Heaven's, no. It's been fun. The whole evening has been fun. Monte Carlo is a fun place, isn't it? And Caroline was quite convinced. She's in love with Jean-Claude, did she tell you?'

'Not in so many words,' he said.

'Well, he's in love with her. He told me so. And I'm sure he'd be good for her.'

He laughed shortly. 'Because he's so—serious, of course.'

He didn't wait for an answer. He went on. 'Since we are indulging in a review of the evening, tell me, did you mean it when you asked me to take you to Monte Carlo again, or was that the loving fiancée playing her part in the play?'

'Did you feel we were acting in a play? That's how it seemed to me too.'

He seemed to ponder that while he pulled in to the side to allow a large coach to pass. Then he said, 'Not all the time,' and he didn't speak again until they stopped outside the villa.

CHAPTER NINE

As THEY got out of the car Josie said, 'I'm going to make some tea now. I'm so thirsty. All that wine with dinner, and liqueur with coffee! Will you join me?'

'No, thanks,' Leon said shortly. 'I've got something to attend to with the car.' He unlocked the door of the villa and walked away.

The curt refusal felt like a slap in the face. Josie's knees began to tremble, and she had to hold on to the worktop while she filled the kettle. She knew she was being oversensitive, but she had thought that if they sat on the terrace and drank tea together she might find out what had made him change suddenly when they left Monte Carlo.

But she had to make tea in a mug, with one tea-bag, and drink it standing up in the kitchen. She washed the mug and put it away. Then she went upstairs to Leon's spare room and collected her bag and the various things she had left there. When all was tidy she went down and unlocked the door of Mon Abri. She didn't quite know why she locked it behind her. Perhaps it was because Leon had suddenly turned into a stranger.

In her bedroom she hung up the yellow dress carefully. It would be a useful addition to her wardrobe, although she had no idea when she would wear it again. In the morning she must settle up with Leon, find out how much he had paid for it and what Gaston had charged for the work he had done on Mon Abri. She took off the emerald ring and put it in its box. It had served its purpose this evening and had saved her pathetic pride, but it wouldn't be wanted again.

She had a dreary feeling that everything was coming to an end. She had allowed herself to dream this evening, but the dream was over now. Leon had shown her that definitely, from the moment they left Monte Carlo, and now she had to pay the price of her self-indulgence. She thought about it as she got ready for bed. What had he meant when he'd said he had enjoyed part of the evening? Which part? She wondered, but could find no answer. Perhaps the morning would bring a clue to his change of mood. It was never any use guessing what Leon's remarks meant, or if he meant them seriously or not.

She was too tired to stay awake worrying about it, and slept soundly. She awakened with a jump to hear the car starting up and driving away. For one terrible moment she thought that Leon was driving out of her life. She jumped out of bed and, still only half awake, scrambled into some clothes and ran down the stairs and into the next-door kitchen. Sunlight was streaming in through the window and there was a note propped against the kettle.

For a moment Josie held her breath, letting it out with a deep sigh of relief as she read, 'Going down to the town. Will bring food back for lunch. LK.'

She picked up the slip of paper and read it through again, but the bold, scribbled words told her nothing about the man who had written them. She folded the note and put it in the pocket of her jeans. It would be the only thing she would have to remember Leon by when this week was over. Sentimental idiot, she accused herself, but that didn't help.

She made coffee and pulled a hunk off a stale baguette, putting it on a plate with butter and jam. When the coffee was ready she carried it all out to the terrace and sat down at the table, wondering what to do until lunch. She considered beginning to sketch out designs and colours for Mon Abri, but that idea, which would have been so fascinating a few days ago, was pointless now that she had decided that she was going to give up the house if Charles confirmed that it was hers when he returned. She thought of telephoning Uncle Seb to tell him the position, but decided against that too. She would have too much explaining to do, and she was sure that Uncle Seb would disapprove of the way she was living, while waiting for Charles to come home and sort everything out.

The sun was getting very hot now, but she was protected by the hanging vines which gave a cool shade to the table.

She was going to miss this place. She had grown to love it in just a few days. She hoped Leon's family, whoever they were, would appreciate it. But it was a waste of time wondering about Leon's family. He didn't intend to tell her anything about them. Better to think about where she would live herself. She had told the bank manager airily that she intended to stay in Menton, but now that seemed out of the question. No, she would return to London, find a flat in a nice district, and settle down to work. She must have a portfolio of drawings to show to customers, or possibly to a studio who might take her on as one of their staff.

The more she thought about it the more dismal the whole of her future seemed. She would be very lonely, that was certain. Her friends from college days had drifted away when her mother had become so ill and needed constant attention. She would make new friends, join clubs or something. And after a long, long time she *might* forget Leon. She sat staring unseeingly down the neglected garden, her eyes brimming with tears, until at last she realised she was doing the one thing she had vowed never to do. She was feeling very sorry for herself.

Resolutely she got up and searched in the utility room for garden tools. She found a light fork and carried it back to the garden. The ground was ironhard, and all her effort only managed to push it about half an inch into the soil. And anyway, she really didn't know which were weeds and which were not. She pulled at the long tendrils that seemed to be choking other plants, but even those were too tough to remove. This wasn't at all like weeding the pretty garden in St John's Wood.

The sun was blazing down on her head and her cotton top was sticking to her but she struggled on doggedly, finding some sort of comfort in the hard manual work but making very little impression on the weeds. Setting her teeth, she grasped a long tendril and pulled as hard as she could. The tendril broke and she fell backwards into a prickly plant and gave a little scream. She was lying on her back and the sun was in her eyes and her head seemed to be going round dizzily. She tried to turn round, but the prickly plant had fastened itself to her back.

She was almost sobbing with frustration when Leon's voice from somewhere above her said angrily, 'What the hell do you think you're doing?'

It was altogether too much. She shaded her eyes with her hand to glare up at him. 'What does it look like?' she snapped. 'I'm lying on my back in something that feels like a gorse bush. And if you were a gentleman you'd help me up.'

He leaned down and scooped her into his arms. For a moment or two, as he carried her up to the terrace, she felt herself pressed against his hard, damp body and her bones turned to water. Then he dumped her, none too gently, in a chair, and stood looking down at her. 'What were you doing out in that heat without a hat, you stupid girl? You deserve to get heatstroke.'

She laid her hand against her damp forehead. 'I think I've got it,' she muttered.

It was shady and almost cool on the terrace. Josie lay back and closed her eyes and tried to pull herself together. The wretched man was right. She had been stupid not to put a hat on when she'd decided to work in the garden.

Leon disappeared and came back with two tall glasses of lemonade with ice clinking in them. He put a glass down before her. 'Drink that,' he ordered.

Josie drank obediently. He was being kind, if grudgingly. When she had finished the drink she felt quite normal again.

'Thank you,' she said. 'That was all I needed.'

He looked hard at her. 'OK, but don't do it again. It gave me a fright, seeing you lying there.' He sat down beside her and tossed back his own drink in two huge gulps, then lay back in his chair. 'That's better,' he said. 'It was like an oven down in Menton.'

Josie took a handkerchief from her pocket to mop her brow and her fingers encountered the ring-box she had put there. She took it out and put it on the table, waiting in silence to say what she had made up her mind to say. He wasn't looking very receptive, but she plunged in. 'I'm sorry to talk finance on a hot day, but there are things we ought to get settled now. I'd like to know how much you spent on my yellow dress and what you paid Gaston for his work on my house.'

'Oh, let it wait,' he muttered, yawning.

'It can't wait,' Josie pressed on. 'We may not have much time together to sort things out. Now Charles is home we might hear any time which of us owns Mon Abri, and then one of us will stay and the other will leave. You said that the villa wouldn't be any use to you unless you could have both houses. That's what you said, wasn't it?'

'Yes, that's what I said.'

He wasn't being much help, but she went on, 'And the ring won't be required again.' She pushed the box across the table.

He roused himself sufficiently to push it back to her. 'One more day,' he said. 'We're going sailing this afternoon.'

'Sailing? What are you talking about?' He closed

his eyes. Maddening man! She grabbed his arm and shook it. 'Just tell me what you mean.'

'Didn't I tell you? We're going sailing.' He yawned again. 'Do you want all the details? Well, I met Glenys Martin in Menton, just back from Paris, and she took me to see their apartment.' He spoke very slowly and deliberately, as if to a child. 'Then we walked down to the marina to see her husband, Andrew, who was doing things to his boat. That resulted in us both being invited to sail with them this afternoon. Is all that quite clear?' He gave a long-suffering sigh.

'Tolerably so.' She pulled a face at him. 'There's one important thing you've forgotten. What do I wear?'

He looked her up and down with narrowed eyes. Then, with a grin, he drawled, 'Just as you are, I should think.'

Her jeans were tight, and almost worn out, and she could feel the thin stuff of her top sticking to her in revealing places. 'Oh, you're useless,' she told him. 'I'll get lunch.' She picked up the plastic bag he had brought in and marched into the kitchen. Well, at least he seemed to have lost his silent mood and was his usual teasing self again.

The phone rang while she was setting out lunch, and she heard Leon speaking and closed the door into the living-room. She always took care not to overhear his phone conversations. They might be with his London office, or they might be with his family.

After a short time he opened the door and walked over to the table. 'Surprise,' he said. 'That was

Charles's PA. Charles got home yesterday. He has been through all the papers referring to Mon Abri, and when he heard that we were both down here he decided to fly down tomorrow morning. So the waiting will be over and we need think no more about it until we hear definitely which of us is the winner. Now, let's have lunch and then we'll have time for a snooze before we start down to meet the Martins.'

Josie had noticed before that anything Leon suggested seemed to happen.

Things turned out just as he had said they would, and at half past two they were driving down the hill to Menton. Josie was wearing loose white cotton trousers and a white cotton top with blue stripes. She had bought this outfit in London, with an idea of a trip round the bay. She remembered such a thing from a holiday she had had with her parents on the Riviera years ago.

Leon was all in navy blue, trousers and a sleeveless vest. Josie thought he looked gorgeous.

She looked up at him provocatively from under her long lashes. 'Will I do?' she asked. 'I'm wearing my hat, you will notice.'

He glanced at her. 'Adorable, as always,' he said.

She looked at the emerald ring on her finger. They were back on their usual terms. It was an unexpected bonus, but she was not going to indulge in dreams again. It was too painful when you woke up.

The Martins' apartment was in a tall, modern block. Leon drove the car into an underground car park and they were sucked up almost silently in a lift to the top floor.

Mrs Martin opened the door and greeted them cheerfully. She looked even younger today, in trousers and a thin nylon jacket, and with her hair brushed back casually and kept in place with a corduroy peaked yachting cap.

'Andrew's down at the boat. Will you go and join him, Leon? Josie and I will follow when I've packed up the tea things.'

'Yes, ma'am.' He saluted smartly and turned back to the lift.

Josie guessed that Mrs Martin had once been a schoolteacher. That particular way of giving orders would never quite leave her. She led Josie into a large, long room with a magnificent view of the harbour. 'We couldn't resist taking this place,' she said when Josie exclaimed with delight at the panoramic view of sea and boats. 'So that Andrew could at least look at boats if he wasn't actually in one. He thinks of nothing else now that he's retired.' She smiled fondly. 'I'll go and pack up. Would you like to see the kitchen?'

Josie followed her hostess into an immaculate kitchen with a wonderful view of the hills behind Menton. 'What a super apartment you have, Mrs Martin.'

'Yes, we were lucky to get it. But please call me Glenys. "Mrs Martin" makes me feel old.'

Josie said, 'Of course, but you don't look at all old.'

'Flatterer!' She chuckled with pleasure. 'But I'm old enough to have a married son, you know. He and his wife lived in Mon Abri until their second baby was coming along. The house was too small for them then. They were able to get a larger flat quite near to us here, so I have the pleasure of seeing my new grandchild and Patrick too. He's a lovely little boy, nearly five now.'

Josie rummaged in her canvas shoulder-bag and brought out the three-legged donkey. 'I wonder if he left this behind when your son moved out of Mon Abri. I found it under the bed in the small bedroom there.'

Glenys took the toy with a little cry of pleasure. 'Donk! Yes, Patrick found he had lost it after they had moved. He'll be overjoyed to see it again. May I keep it?'

'Of course. I was going to make a new leg for it.'

Glenys shook her head. 'No need. A three-legged donkey is a unique personality.'

She put it away in a drawer and said, 'Perhaps Patrick will be able to thank you himself. How long have you planned to stay?'

'I'll be going back to London very soon, I'm afraid.'

'Ah, well, next time you come down we must arrange a tea party—and invite Donk,' Glenys smiled. 'Now I must get on with packing the food.'

She had evidently prepared the food in advance and wrapped each item in greaseproof paper. She packed it all into an oilskin bag, carefully tucking in the flaps. 'It gets a bit wet in the boat sometimes,' she explained. 'Have you got a mac with you?'

'I've brought a plastic mac, one of those things you can tuck away in your pocket,' Josie said. 'I gave it to Leon to look after.'

'That will do splendidly. It isn't going to be a day

for oilskins anyway. But I'm afraid your pretty hat may blow off,' Glenys added. 'I'll lend you one of my caps, if you like.' She took Josie into the bedroom and pulled out a drawer in the chest. 'There you are.' She handed a peaked cap, similar to the one she was wearing, to Josie, who took off the blue sunhat and pulled on the cap.

'It fits beautifully,' she said, admiring herself in a long mirror. 'Thank you, Glenys. It's very kind of you. Now I really feel I'm going sailing.'

There was a slight pause, and then the elder woman said, 'I must apologise. I didn't know when we met a few days ago that you and Leon were engaged to be married. I'm sure you'll both be very happy. You're just the girl for Leon, and you will be able to help him with his difficulties. Poor boy, I thought he looked rather downcast when I met him this morning. He was telling me about the situation with his family, how he was hoping to get the villa ready for them and how you were helping him.' She shook her head slowly. 'What a responsibility for a young man. And that poor girl...' She clicked her tongue in sympathy.

Josie found she was staring at her, her mouth falling open stupidly, and couldn't say a word. But Glenys didn't appear to notice. She lifted Josie's left hand and admired the emerald ring. Then she slung the oilskin bag over her shoulder. 'Shall we go and join the men?' She led the way out to the lift.

As they walked together to the marina Glenys chattered on about her husband and his boat. Josie fixed a smile on her lips and said yes and no in what she hoped were the right places. She was trying to work out why Leon had deliberately told her nothing about his family, which was, after all, the most important part of the situation, when Glenys Martin—whom he hadn't met for years—seemed to know all about it. She was not altogether surprised, for she had guessed now and again that there was something about his family that had brought that look of anxiety to his face, but she couldn't help feeling hurt that he had not chosen to talk to her about it. They were friends, and friends should be able to confide in each other.

For once she was not conscious of her surroundings. Then Leon's voice came from somewhere ahead, and Glenys waved and shouted back.

Josie put puzzling thoughts out of her mind and saw that they were on the concrete walkway of the marina. Leon was standing beside one of the bollards and he lifted a hand in greeting. Josie's heart gave a little leap, as it always did when she first saw him after an absence. Oh, but she loved him, she knew, whether he wanted to tell her about his family or not.

There was a tall, white-haired man standing in the boat moored to the bollard. Glenys introduced him to Josie. 'Josie—Andrew,' she said without formality, and he reached up to shake Josie's hand, smiling and asking her if she enjoyed sailing. She said tactfully that she had never sailed before but she knew she was going to enjoy sailing with him, which brought a beam to his deeply tanned face.

'Good,' he said, and offered a hand to her to help her jump down into the boat. She was followed by Glenys. Finally Leon unwound the rope from the bollard, coiling it up and tossing it into the boat and following it himself. Andrew took his place at the wheel, with Leon standing beside him, and Josie sat with Glenys in one of the seats surrounding the cockpit. There was the sound of a motor starting up and they were off.

Once out of the harbour the red sails were unfurled and bellied out in the following wind. The motor was switched off and the boat was soon cutting through the water at a good rate.

Josie asked where they were going and Glenys said, 'We're going to follow the coast as far as Nice and pull in to have our picnic tea. You'll be able to pick out the places you've visited. There's Monte Carlo in the distance.' She paused, and then went on, 'Leon told me you went to Monte Carlo yesterday to see Caroline.'

'Yes, we had a nice time. Caroline looked lovely.' Josie remembered how Glenys had stiffened up at their first meeting when she spoke of Caroline, and knew she must proceed tactfully.

Glenys sighed heavily. 'Yes, she's a pretty girl. But I do wish she wasn't working in Monte Carlo. It's not the place for a girl, and she'll meet all sorts of undesirable men there. I know she's of age, and she can please herself, but I hate to be on bad terms with her. I suppose I'm old-fashioned; I was brought up rather strictly. Most of the time I lived with my grandparents. My father's job took him abroad for long spells and my mother went with him.' She gave Josie a rueful little smile. 'My grandfather thought gambling was the work of the devil.'

She hesitated, staring out across the water. Then she seemed to make up her mind to confide in Josie.

'You see, Caroline seems to imagine that she's in love with this man who works at the Casino. They even want to get engaged, and she's asking me to invite him to our home so that I can meet him.' She frowned, tipping back her cap and rubbing her brow. 'Somehow I can't agree. It would seem as if I were giving my consent. Every time she comes home we quarrel about it, and it makes me so unhappy.' She sighed, shaking her head. 'You met him yesterday. Do you really think I should bury my prejudice?'

Josie thought for a time, and then said, 'I can't possibly advise you, but if you want my opinion I think you should perhaps meet Jean-Claude. I liked him. I thought he was sincere, and he seemed a steady sort of man.'

Glenys brightened. 'Oh, I'm so glad I asked you. Leon said the same thing this morning, and Andrew just says, "Let's meet the fellow and look him over." But I think a woman's opinion is much more valuable.'

She was silent and thoughtful after that, leaving Josie to revel in the new and exhilarating sensation of being at sea in a small sailing boat. The boat was gathering speed now, sending waves slapping against the side and a little cloud of spray over the rail, leaving a taste of salt on Josie's lips. The sun shone down and seemed as if it would go on shining down on them for ever. The cloudless blue of the sky merged with the blue of the water. Some of Josie's curls escaped from her cap and blew backwards and forwards, tickling her nose. Best of all, she could watch Leon's changing expression as he talked to Andrew.

She drew in a long breath. If this was their last outing it couldn't have been more perfect, and the best of it was that Leon seemed to have shaken off his withdrawn mood. He was chatting away to Andrew, and now and then he turned and smiled at her.

Once or twice nearby boats hailed Andrew, and he shouted back lustily. There were many other boats around, taking advantage of the perfect sailing weather, boats with various coloured sails—blue, white, red, striped. Once Andrew turned to his wife, 'Look, Glenys, there's one of those wing-sail boats.' He pointed, but the boat was too far away for Josie to see clearly. Andrew went on, 'Have you heard of them, Leon? State-of-the-art technology. Everything is done by just a hand on the wheel. They tack, gybe, slow down and stop, turn round, all without any phys-ical effort. Marvellous!'

His wife chuckled. 'I'll put one in your stocking at Christmas,' she said, and they all laughed.

The Martins were a happy couple, Josie thought, and she liked them very much. She hoped the bad feeling with Caroline could be cleared up.

They were sailing close to the coast, and Josie tried to make out Ste-Agnès but the tops of the hills were shrouded in mist. Further on, the twin headlands of Monte Carlo and Monaco came into view, and Leon turned and smiled at Josie and said, 'Remember this?' She could see the Casino, and further on the rock of Monaco, with the palace perched up high on it. Josie smiled back at Leon and nodded. It was sad that they wouldn't go there again together—or anywhere else, she thought, biting her lip to keep the tears from starting up, forgetting that she had vowed to keep this afternoon happy.

Some time later Glenys pointed out Nice, but the town itself was too far away to be seen in detail, for Andrew had steered further from the coast to keep out of the way of boats leaving the harbour.

When they had passed Nice Andrew turned towards the coast. The motor started, the sails were furled and the boat drew in gently to a small inlet with trees along one bank. In a shady place under the trees they dropped anchor.

'We usually have tea here when we come this way,' Glenys told Josie. 'Come down and see the cabin. I'll boil a kettle and make a pot of tea, and we'll take everything up on deck and picnic.'

Just in front of the wheel two or three steps led down to the cabin, which had a drop-leaf table in the middle and two divans.

'With the table-leaf down these convert into comfortable beds,' Glenys said. 'And there's a shower and lavatory through that door, and a kitchenette here. All very compact, you see.'

'It's delightful,' Josie said. 'Like having a beautiful second home by the sea. That's how it would be to me, but of course you have a home by the sea already, you lucky person.'

'Yes, I know I'm lucky. We've been married for thirty years. I can't wish you and Leon anything better.'

Josie murmured something, and turned away to hide her face.

In the tiny kitchenette Glenys put the kettle on to boil while Josie unpacked the oilskin bag and set everything out on a tray on paper plates. Tea was made in a huge pot, and Josie was relieved to see that they were to drink their tea from china cups, and not plastic throw-away mugs, which Glenys said were an insult to a good cup of tea, with which Josie fervently agreed.

They carried the tray and the pot of tea, with milk in a vacuum flask, up to the after-deck, and Andrew found a folding stool to act as a table. The two men sat on the deck and Glenys instructed everyone to help themselves.

Tea was a light-hearted meal. Andrew proved to have a dry wit and told stories of their sailing adventures, which made Josie and Leon splutter with laughter while they munched crusty pieces of baguette spread with pâté. There were crisp little ginger biscuits, and almond-flavoured cakes with cherries on top, slices of melon in one box, and the juiciest strawberries Josie had ever tasted in another.

When the plates were all empty, and the last scraps of food tossed to the squawking birds to fight over, Andrew carried the tray down to the kitchenette, followed by Leon with the huge teapot and milk flask. When they returned Andrew stretched out on the deck to 'repair his energy for the return sail'. He took off his nylon jacket and folded it to put under his head, and in a very few minutes was fast asleep. Leon took the seat beside Josie.

Glenys, on Josie's other side, stood up, saying she had things to attend to in the cabin, smiled at them and departed.

Josie didn't look at Leon. 'She's being tactful,' she said in a low voice. 'I felt so guilty when she said how pleased she was that we were engaged and that I would be such a help to you. This charade gets more and more embarrassing.'

He took one of her hands and held it very tightly. 'Never mind, love,' he said, with a glance at Andrew, who was still fast asleep. 'It won't be long now. This should be our final act in the play.'

Tomorrow she would say goodbye to him. Tears gathered behind her eyelids and she turned her face away. He put his other hand under her chin, turning her head round. 'Tears?' he said softly. 'Why?'

'N-nothing,' she stammered, biting her lower lip hard. 'Just that I'm always sad at the end of anything.' She made a valiant effort to smile. 'Silly, isn't it?'

He put his arm round her and drew her towards him. 'No,' he said softly. 'I'm sad too. It's been such an enjoyable little holiday.'

Andrew soon wakened, sat up and gave a huge yawn. He rubbed his eyes and scrambled to his feet. 'Time to go,' he said. 'Anchors aweigh.' He looked meaningfully at Leon.

'Aye, aye, sir.' Leon took his arm from around Josie's waist and stood up, smiling down at her. 'Enjoying it?' he asked.

She nodded. 'Very much.' Again she had caught a hint of tenderness in his smile. Or had she imagined it?

Glenys appeared from the cabin and took the seat that Leon had left. Leon hauled up the anchor, the motor started, and when they had left the inlet the sails were unfurled.

'The wind will be against us sailing back to Menton,' Glenys told Josie. 'So we'll have to tack— that is, proceed in a zig-zag course. You have to duck down when the boom comes swinging over, otherwise you get a bump on your head.' The boom, she explained, was the wooden bar fixed to the bottom of the mainsail.

On the homeward sail Andrew steered further from the coast, so there was nothing to remark about, and once Josie had mastered the trick of ducking her head when the boom came swinging across she was thankful that Glenys passed the time by talking about her son and his wife and her two beloved grandchildren.

'They were so happy when their second was a girl,' she said. 'She's called Melissa and she's the most delightful child. I have to stop myself from visiting them too often. Grandmothers mustn't push themselves. But Beth, Jonathan's wife, is a very sweet girl and never seems to mind. Jonathan is away a good deal, and I think she is glad of my help to babysit so that she can spend an evening with her friends. They are such a happy little family.' Josie listened to all this with interest, and was glad that Glenys didn't mention her own 'engagement' to Leon.

As they came into the harbour at Menton the motor was switched on and the sails furled, and at last the boat drew safely into its berth. Leon threw up the coiled rope and sprang on to the concrete walkway of the marina to tie up the boat to its bollard. He reached down to help Josie up, and she watched while the boat was made 'ship-shape', as Andrew called it.

Finally they all piled into the Martins' car and drove to the apartment. As they got out of the car Glenys said, 'It's been lovely. I'm so sorry we can't make a day of it and all have dinner together, but Andrew and I have a long-standing engagement. Never mind—next time you're down in Menton we must have a party. Perhaps you'll be married by then. When is it to be?'

Josie said nothing, and Leon drawled, 'Oh, pretty soon,' and gave her a happy smile, which made her want to hit him.

'I'll go and get my hat while you get the car out,' she said in a cool voice. 'Thank you for lending me your cap, Glenys,' she said, taking it off and shaking out her russet curls.

In the end Glenys went up to get Josie's hat while Josie climbed into Leon's car and Andrew took the space vacated.

Leon and Josie drove away to a chorus of thank-yous and a final laughing request from Glenys. 'Don't forget to send us some wedding cake.'

Leon smiled down at Josie as they drove up the hill. 'Tired? It's been a good afternoon, hasn't it?'

'What?' she murmured absently. 'Oh, yes, very good.'

She wasn't thinking of the sail at that moment. She was remembering what Glenys had said about Leon's family. Once again this 'engagement' had put her in a humiliating position, for Glenys would have expected her to know all about it. And Leon should have told her, she argued. Right at the beginning, when she had asked him why he was so anxious to have Mon Abri. He had merely said 'for my family'. Why hadn't he been straight with her then?

Now she had to decide whether to tackle him about it or to let the matter pass without comment.

She had a sinking, unreasonable feeling that on her decision rested her whole future happiness.

CHAPTER TEN

LEON'S voice broke in on her debate with herself. 'Would you like to go out to dinner? There's nothing interesting in the house, is there? And I feel like a good meal. Sailing always gives me an appetite. How about you?'

She couldn't tackle him about his family if they were sitting across a restaurant table. And she could hardly do it when they got back either, after he had treated her to a meal. It was a relief to have her mind made up for her.

'Yes, thank you, I'd love to,' she said. 'Although I shouldn't, after that enormous tea.'

He was turning the car into the drive. He parked and switched off the ignition. Then he turned sideways in his seat and looked at her, an odd expression in his eyes. 'Excellent,' he said. 'I was afraid you might refuse.'

'Were you? Why?'

'Well, this is likely to be our last evening together, and I suppose it isn't really cause for celebration.'

'It is, for one of us,' she said brightly.

He nodded. 'What a pity we can't both win.'

'Oh, but then there wouldn't have been a game,' she said. 'There has to be a winner in any game.'

'Game? Is that how you've seen it?'

She thought for a moment. 'Well—yes. We decided

at the beginning that we were stuck here in our separate houses, and that we couldn't fight all the time until Charles came and set things straight. So we would be friends. That was your suggestion, and it was just as well, for friends help each other. And if I hadn't wakened you up and told you to turn off the water I might have been drowned.'

He was grinning now. 'Yes, and if you hadn't been around to bind up my wound I might have bled to death. So it was useful to be friends, wasn't it?'

She sighed. 'What a long time ago it seems, and yet it isn't a week yet since we had our first fight.'

He turned and got out of the car, walking quickly round the front to open her door. 'It isn't very friendly to remind me of that,' he said.

She gave a little gurgle of laughter. 'Ah, no, but that was before we became friends.'

'Wretched girl! I refuse to argue with you. Come along.' He took her hand, threading his fingers with hers, and they walked round to the terrace.

She could feel the electricity that ran between their clasped hands and up her arm. She wondered if Leon felt it too. She thought perhaps he did, for when he let her go he drew in a sharp breath.

Her knees were shaking as she groped in her canvas bag for her key.

'We'll meet here when we're both ready,' he said. 'Can you manage your shower, or would you like to borrow mine?'

She thanked him and said she felt sure she could manage. She had had one or two practice sessions with the shower.

Her knees were still shaking as she let herself in to Mon Abri, and she sat down in a chair for a few minutes until she could pull herself together.

Talking about the game they had been playing might have been an opportunity to ask him why he had deliberately told her nothing about his family, but of course she couldn't ask him. The thought appalled her now, and she wished that Glenys hadn't mentioned it.

But there was something else she must talk to him about. This evening was to be a celebration for Leon, although he didn't know that yet, and she must tell him what she had decided to do about selling Mon Abri if Charles confirmed that it really did belong to her. Should she tell Leon today, or wait until Charles arrived tomorrow? She ran a hand through her curls. What a muddle everything was! Better to act on the impulse of the moment.

But as she made her way slowly upstairs one thing loomed before her, so huge and black and frightening. She was going to say goodbye tomorrow to Leon, to her love. And she wasn't sure how she was going to bear it.

In the shower-room, Josie stripped off her clothes and contemplated the array of taps. More by good luck than anything else she managed to produce a beautiful tepid spray, and stepped under it quickly in case it stopped. But it continued as it was, without freezing her or scalding her, and she made the most of it, relaxing under the soothing caress of the cool water on her hot body.

As she dried herself with the fleecy pink towel that

Leon had brought from Menton at her request, she remembered that she hadn't yet found out how much she owed him.

In the bedroom she put on clean undies, and then surveyed the limited number of dresses in the wardrobe. She would wear the cream dress, she decided. It was more suitable for an evening out than the sundresses.

As she towelled her hair dry she felt a strange sense of excitement, as if she had just met Leon and this was their first date instead of their last. But she wouldn't dwell on the inevitable parting. She was going to enjoy this evening.

She combed out her curls as best she could, with only the tiny mirror to help her, and then slipped the dress carefully over her head, zipping up the back with the ancient buttonhook she kept for the purpose. She put on a light make-up to lips and eyes. Already her face and arms were nicely tanned. She gave careful attention to her hands and applied natural varnish to her nails. Pushing her feet into white sandals, she ran down to the terrace.

Leon was there before her, and her heart missed a beat because he looked so handsome in his white tuxedo, his black hair damp from his shower and curling slightly into his neck.

As she came towards him he took both her hands in his, holding her away to look her slowly up and down.

'Lovely!' he pronounced. 'Your eyes are green tonight. And you're still wearing my ring. Thank you for that.'

She released her hand and looked down at the ring. 'I meant to take it off. I'm afraid it's become a habit.' She started to pull the ring off her finger but he covered her hand with his. 'Wear it tonight,' he said. 'Just to please me.'

'Or until the referee arrives to announce the winner of the game?'

'No,' he said. 'The game's over. We'll say what we mean from now on. Although,' he added, 'I must say I've enjoyed being engaged.'

She laughed lightly. 'It has been good practice for when you are really engaged.'

He wasn't smiling as he replied heavily, 'That day will be a long time off, I'm afraid.'

There was an awkward silence. Then Leon said, 'We'd better get going and find a good restaurant that isn't too full.'

After one or two false stars in Menton he found a small restaurant overlooking a flower-filled park, and installed Josie at a table in the cosy bar on the ground floor while he went to park the car. He returned after a few minutes and handed her a small cardboard box.

She opened it to disclose a perfect little orchid, its curled petals shading from cream to green.

She exclaimed with delight. 'Leon, thank you. It's simply perfect. Will you pin it on for me, please?'

He leaned down to pin the flower to the shoulder of her dress, then stepped back to study the effect. 'Yes,' he said. 'It just matches your eyes.'

'But my eyes aren't green.'

'They are when you're excited. You can't see them yourself, you know.'

'Oh, dear,' Josie said, 'I'll have to be careful.'

'Not with me. I enjoy watching them.'

'Is that why you tease me? To watch me getting angry?'

'No, don't accuse me of that. Now, what will you have to drink?'

'Lime, please, a nice long one.'

He went over to the bar and came back with a tall glass of lime for her and Scotch for himself. He held the glass up before he put it down for her. 'This goes with your eyes too.'

He sat down next to her, smiling the rare smile that she loved. 'Well, of course I'm excited,' she said. 'It's a long time since I've been out to dinner with an attractive man. And I think you've spiked my lime.'

'Just a drop or two of gin,' he confessed, meeting her accusing look blandly. 'To get the party off to a good start.'

They dined upstairs, on a balcony overlooking the flower garden. The scent of roses drifted upon the warm air and Josie said, 'Everywhere you go in Menton there seem to be flowers. I'm sure it would lift the spirits of anyone from a town.'

She thought Leon's face darkened, but at that moment a waiter approached with a large menu card. They consulted it together and settled on lobster salad followed by *poussin rôti* with *pommes frites*. Leon asked for the wine list. 'A good selection,' he said, running a long finger down the list. 'But I think a celebration calls for champagne, don't you?'

Josie had made up her mind to tell Leon tonight what she had decided to do about Mon Abri, but it was not until they had finished eating the delectable meal and the bottle of champagne was almost empty that the moment arrived. Leon half-filled both their glasses and held his up. 'We haven't drunk a toast to the winner of the game yet,' he said.

Josie lifted her glass. 'I will give the toast,' she said. 'To the winner of the game—Mr Leon Kent. I'm afraid you can't drink this toast yourself.' She sipped her wine, her eyes challenging him.

Leon was staring at her, dumbfounded, his glass halfway to his mouth. He put the glass down. 'You've had too much champagne, my girl. You're not seeing straight.'

'I'm seeing perfectly straight,' she said. 'I've wanted to talk to you about this for some time, and tonight seems a good time. When Charles arrives, I must first confirm that Mon Abri does indeed belong to me, and if it does I shall tell him that I've decided not to keep it but to sell, either to you or to him, which ever is best.'

He was regarding her through narrowed eyes. 'Only yesterday you were weeping because I was pencilling out your little house on the plan. You told me then how much you had been thrilled to get it and how you were looking forward to refurbishing it. What has happened to make you change your mind?'

'You don't look very pleased,' she said as he put his glass down on the table.

'Has someone been talking to you about this? Glenys Martin, for instance? She's a talkative lady.'

'Certainly not.' It was only half a lie. 'I've been

thinking a lot about it lately, and there are various reasons why I've made the decision.'

'Such as?' His eyes still held hers steadily.

'Well—I've been doing some sums, and I've found that it would take far more than I'm prepared to spend to put Mon Abri in good order. Then—oh, I should have new neighbours whom I might not get along with.'

'And?' There was a grimness about his mouth now.

She met his eyes straight as she replied, 'Although you've never told me why you want the house so badly, I can guess that your need is greater than mine, and since we are friends that naturally weighs with me. Now are you satisfied?'

She was still watching his face, and saw his mouth gradually curve into a wry smile. 'I can't quite believe it yet, but if it is all as you say, I'm more than satisfied. I'm delighted. I feel as if a weight has been lifted from my back, and all I can say is thank you, my friend. Here's to you.' He lifted his glass again and drank the contents at a gulp.

Their eyes met across the table and held, and Josie couldn't look away. It was Leon who broke the silence, saying, 'I want to tell you about my family. I can do that now. But not here. Perhaps when we get back to the villa.'

Josie nodded. She guessed that he wanted to remember their last evening together as a happy time. She had crème de menthe with her coffee 'because it will match your eyes'. He had a small brandy, and then called for the bill.

The car was parked on the roadside, quite close to

the restaurant, and Leon drove back up the hill to the villa but passed the gate to the drive.

'Where are we going?' Josie asked.

'Higher up, so that we can stop and look at the lights down below,' Leon told her. After a few more minutes he turned the car and backed into a verge beside the road. He switched off the engine. 'There,' he said. 'The lights of Menton. Not quite up to Monte Carlo standards.'

Josie chuckled as she looked down at the wide view spread below. 'I like it better. It's more friendly.' There were lights everywhere. Fairy lights looped up and twinkled all along the sea front, and further out at sea, tiny pinpoints of light showed where boats were bobbing at anchor. In the Old Town, glowing windows led up to the beautiful church, with its bell-tower, flood-lit and standing out against the sky. The warm honey colour of the stone was just visible in the velvety blackness of the Mediterranean night. This was something else that she would remember when she was back in her London flat.

Leon flicked up the seat-arm between them and moved nearer to her. He took her hand in his, saying, 'I want to tell you now something I didn't want you to know earlier. It will explain why I am so keen on getting Mon Abri to make a home for my family.' He paused, looking down at their joined hands.

'My father died about eighteen months ago. My mother, as I told you, is French, and was brought up in Menton. She always wanted to come back and live here when my father retired, but when he died rather suddenly she felt that she preferred to stay in London to be near my sister, who has three small sons. Then, three months ago, my sister Kate and her husband were in a car crash coming home from an evening out with friends. Neil died later in hospital, and Kate was injured so badly that at first they thought she wouldn't recover.'

He drew in a quick breath, and when he went on spoke in a deliberately flat voice. 'I took things over, of course. I found a nanny for the boys—the twins, who are four, and the youngest, who is not yet two— and moved Maman into Kate's flat to be near the hospital and to be there when—if—Kate came home. In time Kate recovered, thank God, but they do not know if she will walk again. Maman is there to look after her, of course, and the nanny lives in. But they are all crammed together in a smallish flat and Maman and I consulted about what should be done.

'Then I met Charles, and he told me about the villa here and assured me that he was only waiting for the deeds of Mon Abri and then I would be able to purchase it and convert it into a home for all of them. Maman was thrilled, and, as you know, I purchased the villa straight away. I was just waiting to complete the purchase of Mon Abri when you appeared on the scene.'

There was a long silence while Josie took all this in. Then she said, 'But I don't understand. Why didn't you tell me this before?'

He gave a bitter little laugh. 'Isn't it obvious? I knew your soft heart, my love, and that if I came to you with a sob story, you'd agree immediately that Mon Abri should be mine, even if it turned out to belong to you. It would feel like emotional blackmail.'

He had called her his love! Her heart began to behave crazily. Then he went on, 'That's why I told you that I wouldn't be able to pass on the ring to any girl for a long, long time. How could I have the nerve to ask any girl to marry me and share the burden that would be all I could offer?'

Josie drew her hand from his. She felt a creeping iciness all over her body.

'No,' she said, 'I suppose you couldn't. But if she loved you?' she added in a small voice.

He shook his head and said bitterly, 'Then I should have to watch her being slowly disillusioned. I still have my way to make as an architect, as well as being responsible for my family.'

He put an end to the conversation by switching on the ignition and the headlights. As they drove back down the hills, Josie turned away in her seat for a moment, slipped off the ring and put it in the box which she had been keeping in her bag. When they arrived back at the villa Leon locked the car and they walked round to the terrace.

'I may as well go to bed now,' Josie said, trying to keep the unhappiness from her voice.

'Oh, no, we must have our final drink together,' Leon told her firmly. 'You like to drink tea on these occasions, I seem to remember. Sit down out here and I'll make tea.' He went into the kitchen.

As they drank their tea Leon talked about sailing, and how he would like to have a boat here some day. Josie listened and tried to look interested, but the thought of what he would do here 'some day' when she wouldn't be here was infinitely depressing, and when they finished their tea and Leon had stacked up the tray and taken it back to the kitchen she stood up, determined to go off to bed and be alone. She waited for a moment, looking through the trail of vines down the garden. The moon had come up, and in its pale light the garden no longer looked overgrown and neglected, but rather beautiful.

Leon came up behind her and put both hands on her shoulders, turning her round to face him. 'Well met by moonlight, fair Titania,' he said with a chuckle.

Josie summoned up a laugh. 'Your Shakespeare is a little rusty, Mr Kent,' she told him.

'Is it? Please put me right.'

'It should be "Ill met by moonlight, proud Titania,"' she told him. 'You see, the queen had stolen the king's favourite page-boy, and he was very cross with her.'

'Oh, dear, we can't have that,' he said. 'I shall have to compose the lines myself. How about, Well met by moonlight, lovely Josephine?' His hands slipped down from her shoulders to her waist and he drew her towards him. 'And you are indeed lovely, Josie.' His voice was low and husky, and she knew she should pull away but was powerless to do so, and when his head bent down to hers her bones felt as if they were melting and her arms went up round his neck to pull him closer.

He kissed her gently at first, and then more passionately, and she kissed him back, showing him shamelessly how much she cared.

When he drew away at last she waited, holding her breath.

'I'm sorry,' he said slowly. 'I shouldn't have done that. But friends may kiss, you know. And now you'd better go to bed. Goodnight, Josie.'

'Goodnight, Leon,' she replied. 'I'd better give you back your ring now.' She unfastened her bag, took out the little box and put it down on the table, and walked away from him. She unlocked her door with damp, shaking hands, climbed the stairs, holding on to the rail, and managed to reach her bedroom before her knees buckled under her and she fell on the bed and sobbed until she had no more tears to shed.

Much later she bathed her face, got into her nightie and crawled into bed. She had expected to lie awake all night, but instead she was asleep, tired out, very quickly.

She wakened to sunshine making bright bars on the shutters, and lay trying to remember what was happening. Then, quite suddenly, her mind cleared and she remembered everything. Today Charles was coming, and today she would say goodbye to Leon and go back to London with Charles. There was a hard lump in her chest, and she rubbed it as if she could clear it away. She had to bite her lip hard to stop herself dissolving into tears again. She must carry off the final moments with something like dignity.

Her watch told her it was after ten o'clock, but she didn't hurry over dressing. It was already getting very hot, so she had a cooling shower and dressed in a

clean sundress, with a flower pattern of pink and
green against a white background. She brushed her
curls out and let them form a halo round her face,
made up her eyes with faint green shadow and walked
slowly downstairs.

When she had nearly reached the bottom she realised that Leon was speaking on the phone in the room
next door and stood still. He must have put the call
through himself, for she hadn't heard the phone ring.
She guessed that he was telling his mother the good
news, and heard the last words before she could move
out of hearing distance.

'Yes, she told me yesterday that she agreed. I knew
you'd be glad to know straight away. Oh—it was a
bit sticky at first, but my well-known charisma carried
the day. Yes—good—I'll say goodbye now. No, I'm
fine, and so is Josie. I'll tell her what you say.'
Silence. He had hung up.

So—all this time he had been intent on charming
her so that finally she would agree to his having Mon
Abri, as she had done yesterday.

It was just as she had feared at first. Then things
had changed and she had believed him sincere. She
felt icy cold, but stiffened herself and walked down
the remaining steps and on to the terrace.

Leon came towards her, smiling. 'That was
Caroline on the phone,' he said. 'I've been telling her
how her mother told me yesterday that she had decided to put her prejudice aside and invite Jean-
Claude to dinner. As you can guess, Caroline was
over the moon, and she asked me particularly to thank
you for your part in persuading Glenys to be reason-

able. She told me all about her difficulty when we were in Monte Carlo, and I promised to do what I could to help her. So there's a happy ending for them. Will you have breakfast? I've had mine, but I could make you some coffee, and I got some fresh croissants this morning.'

Josie sank into a chair. How she had misjudged him! She felt shattered and guilty, but she couldn't tell him. 'I'm very late, I'm afraid, but I'd love some coffee,' she said. 'Nothing else, thank you.' She had to bite her lip hard to stop herself bursting into tears again.

When Leon came back with coffee she thanked him and said, 'But you shouldn't wait on me.'

'Rubbish, I'd do far more than that for you, you know.' Their eyes met and she thought, I can't bear this. I must get away.

And at that moment there was the sound of a car on the drive and Leon hurried out.

Josie put a hand to her throat. This was the beginning of the end, then, and she had to carry it off without losing control of herself.

Leon came back a few minutes later with Charles beside him. Charles looked very handsome in a white linen suit with a sapphire-blue open-neck shirt. He beamed upon Josie as she greeted him. 'You're looking prettier than ever, poppet.'

'And *you're* looking very pleased with yourself.' She patted his cheek affectionately. 'Although you have no right to be—keeping Leon and me working ourselves into nervous breakdowns before you bother to come back and tell us who Mon Abri belongs to.'

'I know, I know,' Charles said contritely. 'I've already grovelled to Leon, and now I'll grovel to you, Jo. When I heard you were both here I had to come down straight away and clear things up. To my shame, I've quite enjoyed the trip. I had a car waiting at the airport and the drive here from Nice is quite spectacular. Phoo! It's hot. May I take my jacket off?' He pulled off his jacket and sank into a chair at the table where Josie had been drinking her coffee.

Leon said, 'A long cold drink, Charles? How about gin and lime?' He carried the tray back to the kitchen and returned with a tall glass, which Charles emptied in three gulps.

'That's better.' He smiled at them both. 'Now, we must come to business,' he said. 'I'm ashamed to admit that I had forgotten that Mon Abri had been bought by Josie's mother. It was a long time ago, but as soon as I began to go through the books it was clear to me. I checked with Sebastian, Josie, and received a rather curt confirmation.' He grinned. 'I've never been Sebastian's favourite person. Well, to continue—what can be done to please everyone, as you own the main villa, Leon, and Josie owns Mon Abri? The easiest thing is for me to buy Mon Abri from you, Jo, and fix you up with another property, which you might like even better.'

He took a folded sheet of paper from the pocket of his jacket, hanging on the back of his chair. 'See how you like this,' he said, handing it to her. 'It's rather a delightful little place, not far from here, further down the hill. You could have a look at it this afternoon, if you like.'

Josie unfolded the sheet and saw a picture of a small house, half hidden in the trees. There were agent's details beneath the picture, but she didn't bother to read them.

'I would meet the difference in price myself, if you agree to the change.'

She put the paper on the table. 'I'd have to think about it,' she said, glancing at Leon, who was leaning back in his chair, his eyes half closed, seeming to take no interest in the conversation.

Charles stood up. 'I'll leave the two of you to fix things between you. And now, if you have a spare bed, I'd very much like to have a rest.'

Leon got up immediately. 'Of course, I'll take you upstairs. You must have been doing a lot of travelling.'

'*And* it's so tiring getting married again,' Josie teased him, making herself smile. 'What have you done with your new wife?'

'Left her at home,' Charles admitted, pulling a face. 'I reckoned your troubles had to be sorted out first, and Gabrielle has lots of friends in London. But I must get straight back to her, as soon as you two have made up your minds. So I'm afraid I can't stay. I'll drive back to Nice later this morning and take the first plane.'

Josie looked at Leon. 'I told you Charles was getting himself married in America, didn't I?'

Leon shook hands with Charles and congratulated him. Then he led the way upstairs to his spare bedroom.

When he came down again he sank into his chair

and picked up the agent's leaflet from the table. 'Looks a charming little place,' he said, glancing at Josie uncertainly. 'What do you think?'

She shook her head decidedly. 'No, I don't want to stay in Menton. I shall go back to London with Charles, and stay with him and my new stepmother until I find myself a pleasant flat. And now I'd better go up and pack my bag, and be ready when Charles has had his rest.'

Leon nodded, and Josie knew she couldn't speak again. Her throat felt so choked up.

In the bedroom she packed her bag, folding the new yellow dress carefully, although she would never wear it again. She still owed Leon money, but she couldn't possibly go down and talk to him about that. She would ask Charles to repay the debt when next he met Leon. She walked over to the window and stood looking down blindly at the view spread out below, remembering that it was here that she had fallen in love with Mon Abri and determined to keep it for herself. She turned her back on the view and stood in the middle of the room, breathing deeply, willing herself to do what had to be done. When she could no longer put it off she picked up the travelling bag and, with a last look round the empty room, walked slowly downstairs and carried the bag to the front door of the villa. Then she came back to the terrace.

Leon was still sitting where she had left him. 'Goodbye, Leon,' she said, holding out her hand. 'I'll wait for Charles in the car. You can tell him what we've decided when he comes down.'

Leon stood up and took her hand in his, holding it

very tightly so that she couldn't pull away, 'Don't go, Josie,' he said in a low, rough voice. 'I can't bear to let you go.' They stared into each other's eyes. 'You know what I have to offer. Will you take me on? I love you to distraction.' He spoke so low that she could scarcely hear the words.

A miracle had happened and the heavy lump in her throat was slowly dissolving.

She couldn't speak, but it was all there in her eyes as she smiled mistily up at him, breathing his name.

He sank into his chair and pulled her down on to his knees, kissing her over and over, her lips, her eyes, her neck. His head buried in the curve of her shoulder, he drew the ring-box from his pocket and felt for the ring inside.

He lifted his head and smiled at her, the smile that she loved but had thought never to see again. Then he took her left hand and replaced the ring on the third finger. 'It looks more at home there,' he said, lifting her hand to his lips. 'But you haven't told me you love me.'

She curled up closer in his arms. 'Oh, Leon, darling, darling, I love you to distraction too. I've loved you for what seems ages. And you won't have to watch me being—what was it?—slowly disillusioned, I promise.'

After a very long time Josie sat up and said practically, 'What are we going to do, and what do we tell Charles when he comes down?'

Leon thought it over for perhaps one minute, then he said, 'We break our news to him, and when he has got over the shock we all go down and look at the small house.' He touched the agent's brochure on the table. 'If we like it we'll take it for our own second home. We'll call it *Notre* Abri instead of Mon Abri.' They both laughed and kissed again. 'Then, my love, you will return to London with Charles and I will stay here for a couple of days and get the builders started. After which I will return to London, and introduce you to Maman and the family, who will love you. We'll get married there as soon as possible, after which you and I will return here and take up residence in Notre Abri until the building work here is finished and we can move the family down. How's that for a scenario?'

'Lovely,' she said, half delirious with happiness. When Leon planned something it always happened just as he said it would.

This was a dream scenario. And, blissfully, as she heard Charles coming downstairs, and they stood up, hand in hand, to meet him, she knew that this dream was going to come true.

HARLEQUIN ◆ PRESENTS®

HARLEQUIN PRESENTS
men you won't be able to resist
falling in love with...

HARLEQUIN PRESENTS
women who have feelings
just like your own...

HARLEQUIN PRESENTS
powerful passion in
exotic international settings...

HARLEQUIN PRESENTS
intense, dramatic stories that will keep you
turning to the very last page...

HARLEQUIN PRESENTS
The world's bestselling romance series!

Harlequin® Historical

From rugged lawmen and
valiant knights to defiant heiresses
and spirited frontierswomen,
Harlequin Historicals will
capture your imagination with
their dramatic scope, passion
and adventure.

Harlequin Historicals…
they're too good to miss!

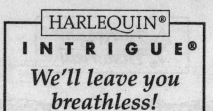

LOOK FOR OUR FOUR FABULOUS MEN!

Each month some of today's bestselling authors bring
four new fabulous men to Harlequin American Romance.
Whether they're rebel ranchers, millionaire power brokers
or sexy single dads, they're all gallant princes—and
they're all ready to sweep you into lighthearted fantasies
and contemporary fairy tales where anything is possible
and where all your dreams come true!

You don't even have to make a wish…
Harlequin American Romance will grant your every desire!

Look for Harlequin American Romance
wherever Harlequin books are sold!

S HARLEQUIN SUPERROMANCE®

...there's more to the story!

Superromance. A *big* satisfying read about unforget-
table characters. Each month we offer
four very different stories that range from family
drama to adventure and mystery, from highly emotional stories to romantic comedies—and
much more! Stories about people you'll
believe in and care about. Stories too
compelling to put down....

Our authors are among today's *best* romance writ-
ers. You'll find familiar names and
talented newcomers. Many of them are
award winners—and you'll see why!

If you want the biggest and best
in romance fiction, you'll get it
from Superromance!

Available wherever Harlequin books are sold.